He smiled. "I'm going to be blunt now, so brace yourself."

"All right." She wasn't sure whether to be happy or scared.

"In spite of the *unusual* circumstances we've found ourselves in today, we seem to like each other. I enjoy your company, and I can barely remember the last time I could say that about a woman. So, my idea would give us some time to explore a friendship, maybe more. I could stay in the cottage, and you could stay in the manor."

Olivia paused. "Your plan…hmm. To be honest, a spaghetti strainer has fewer holes. But…"

"But?"

"Okay, for now, it'll do." She reached out to shake his hand. "You have a deal, Mr. Bromfeld."

"Good." Noah shook her hand, but held it for a moment longer than he needed to.

What was she getting herself into? Perhaps something lovely, something she'd waited her whole life for and didn't even know it. It was so hard to know the ending of a story on the first chapter.

ANITA HIGMAN

Bestselling and award-winning author Anita Higman has thirty-two books published (several coauthored) for adults and children. She's been a Barnes & Noble "Author of the Month" for Houston and has a BA degree, combining speech communication, psychology and art. Anita loves good movies, exotic teas and brunch with her friends. Please visit her online at www.anitahigman.com.

ANITA HIGMAN
Home at Last

HEARTSONG
PRESENTS

LOVE INSPIRED BOOKS

ISBN-13: 978-0-373-48687-8

HOME AT LAST

www.Harlequin.com

Printed in U.S.A.

Many waters cannot quench love;
rivers cannot wash it away.
—*Song of Solomon* 8:7

To my husband, Peter.
Thank you for reminding me daily
why home is such a wonderful place to be.

Chapter 1

Olivia Lamington wriggled the key into the lock of the manor's heavy front door, but it didn't fit quite right—just as her own irregular life had never slipped easily into this world. Especially now. It had been three months since Finney's passing, though her heart still felt the weight of her employer's absence. What a turn of events it had been for her—imagine—an orphan becoming heiress to a castle. She'd embraced the manor as her home, as Finney had requested, but sometimes it still felt as though she were playing house.

The hinges of the door groaned and echoed through the entry hall, making Olivia wither. Although Bromfeld Manor was filled with antiques, tapestries and paintings, it was empty of Finney's scents and sounds. His joy. After twenty years in Finney's employment, how would she live her life now? Was God still smiling down on her?

Not wanting to go inside just yet, she turned back toward the live oaks. The canopy of leaves shimmered, looking like lacework against the afternoon sun, and the branches stretched across the lane as if straining to embrace each other. The breeze tickled her cheeks, making her eyelids flutter shut. The smell of Carolina jasmine filled the air. Oh, how Finney loved springtime in the country, especially his little corner of the world in Southeast Texas. So vivacious and expectant, he would always say.

The sun dipped behind the clouds, darkening the landscape. The shadows reminded her once again how alone she was.

Music, far away and sweetly melancholy, came in on the breeze. In the distance a stranger, who looked about her own age—perhaps somewhere near forty—plodded toward the manor, playing a harmonica. She recognized the folk song, "Danny Boy." With each grinding step his shoes stirred up puffs of clay-colored dust. Had the man's car broken down, or was he homeless? The moment the man noticed Olivia, he stopped as if she were a skittish bird he might frighten off.

He was right. She backed away into the house and locked the dead bolt. The man was a stranger, after all, and with the staff recently dismissed, she was truly alone.

Olivia hurried to one of the front windows, pulled the drape back and studied the man. A stray dog she'd befriended over the months—one she'd named Mops—

latched on to his pant leg, snarling and generally causing him grief. The stranger didn't seem to mind the
tug-of-war, but he did look weary in a thousand other
ways—as though he was on the last journey of his life.

Believing that the stranger would ring the bell, Olivia
scurried into the sunroom so she wouldn't be tempted
to answer the door. She found a book on the shelf—
The Man Who Would Be King—and opened it to the
first page. A pressed flower fluttered out of the novel
and onto the floor, one she'd forgotten about. But then
pressing wildflowers into books and hoping they would
fall out later to delight a reader was her "thing." Or as
Rudyard Kipling might have said, "a trifling custom."
It was so much a part of her that many of the Bromfeld
Manor books held hidden blossoms. She picked up the
translucent bluebonnet and set it on the table.

Just as she expected, the doorbell rang. She sat still.
Olivia, you will not answer that door. She tried to con-
centrate on the first line of the novella, but it was no
use. She ended up going over and over the same words,
waiting for the bell again. When it rang, Olivia jumped.
Then the goofy thing ding-donged five more times.
Who did the man think he was?

Olivia waited, holding her breath. Finally, there was
quiet again. He must have given up. But a moment later
when she turned toward the west end of the room, the
stranger stood by the windows, staring at her through
the glass.

Olivia's book made a flying leap before slapping
back down onto the wood floor. She let out a shriek
so bone rattling that it frightened the stranger, making

him stumble backward. He let out an equally impressive yelp as the big-thorned rosebushes devoured him.

Was he a thief? A murderer? Maybe he'd heard of Finney's death and somehow knew she was alone. *God help me!* What could she do? Call the local sheriff? But there was no time. And Finney had never kept guns on the premises. If she had a gun she'd probably just shoot her foot off with the silly thing, anyway.

Glancing at each of the sunroom windows, she noticed one of them had been left open. Olivia ran to the spot and, with quaking hands, slammed the window shut, locked it and backed away until she hit the wall. Finding a broom behind the door, she grabbed it and held it in front of her as a weapon.

No sound came from the man and no thrashing about in the bushes. Had he been knocked out, or was he playing dead like a sly fox?

After another second or two, muffled words erupted from the rosebushes. "I am Finney Bromfeld's son, Noah," he hollered.

Olivia's mind tore into a dozen questions at once. He couldn't be Finney's son; Finney's son was dead.

The stranger tried to get his footing as he clambered out of the bushes. When he finally straightened, he held out a pink rose like a repentant schoolboy. "So, do you believe me?" He spoke loudly to be heard through the glass.

"I don't know what to think. You don't look anything like Finney." The man had long brown hair, light olive skin and a boring kind of nose. Nothing at all like

Finney, who'd had blond hair, a schnozzle with angles and skin as pink as a newborn mole.

"That's because I resemble my mother," he said.

"Why don't I believe you?" Olivia stepped forward, still aiming the broom at him. "By the way, you scared the woozoos out of me, peeping in the window like that." She sharpened her tone, making it as unpleasant as a paper cut—a nasty one.

"Woozoos? That's a good one." He didn't even bother to squelch his laugh. "Actually, I wasn't *peeping*. I was about to open a window so I could climb in." Then the man stuck the rose into the lapel of his jacket and gave it a pat. "And *you* were the one guilty of gawking out at me from the front window."

Humph. That wasn't the same thing, but to say the obvious seemed ridiculous.

At least the barbed bushes, which had been planted near the windows to discourage thieves, had done their job. His hands and face were scratched up, and his T-shirt and jacket were dirtied. A trickle of blood drizzled down the man's cheek from a small wound on his temple. Olivia's heart softened toward him—but only a mouse's portion. "Before I even think about letting you in…tell me something unique about your family, something only Finney's son might know."

"All right." The man scrubbed his stubble-covered chin. "When I was seventeen my mother was…" He frowned and shook his head as if he'd changed his mind about telling her.

"Was what?"

"My mother was struck by lightning." He crossed his arms. "So, will that do?"

"Maybe." Finney had talked about the incident some years ago. Olivia gave up the idea that the man was a thief and motioned toward the front of the house. "Okay, I will let you in but *not* through the window. Please go around to the front door."

Mops trotted up to the man and growled with more gumption this time.

Hmm. Could have used you a few moments ago.

The man tapped on the glass. "Could you please call off your dog?"

Olivia hesitated, since maybe Mops sensed a danger she wasn't aware of.

Then, with the shameless audacity of a burglar, the man lifted one of the windows and stepped inside the sunroom. "Ever since I was five that lock has never worked right." He stood inside now, dusting off his clothes. "Weren't you tired of shouting through the glass? I was." He looked at her broom and raised his hands as if he were being held up by a loaded gun. Then he grinned.

It was a good smile as smiles go—a fine specimen— but she still wanted to slap it right off his face and maybe leave a stinging red imprint on his cheek to remind him not to go around frightening women.

He cocked his head. "You're not going to scream again, are you?"

"I don't think so."

"Or sweep me to death?" He gestured toward the

broom—the one she still gripped as if her hands were welded to the handle.

Olivia slowly lowered her weapon and then dropped it cold, letting it make a spiteful clatter on the wood floor. She tried not to stare at him, but she gave up and stared anyway. His wild locks were pulled back in a ponytail. My, my, my. She'd never personally met a man with long hair before. Kind of sixties. Noah wasn't terribly handsome, not short or tall, heavy or thin, but he was appealing with his dark eyes darting about, taking in the whole world at once. The man was a dreamer type—one could see that in a moment—but even with all his swashbuckling Johnny Depp air there was a tortured look about him.

And the man had no sense of personal space, since he came up to her and edged a bit too close. "Technically speaking, *you're* the stranger in *my* house."

Confused, Olivia backed away. The scent of him— weeds and wet dog—lingered in her nose. Not the best combo.

"I'm Noah, but I guess I said that back there in the shrubs."

"You did."

"By the way, you have a blight on your roses, and they're in desperate need of pruning. If you're not careful, they're going to forget how to bloom."

"They just need a bit of love." Like a kite coming down to earth, Olivia reeled herself back in. "You're bleeding." She pointed to his cheek.

"My father's roses were always unforgiving…as were so many other things about this home." Noah pulled a handkerchief from an inner pocket and dabbed at his face.

"I'm Olivia Lamington. Like the little coconut-covered sponge cakes in Australia."

"I've been to Australia, and since I have a great fondness for those little coconut-covered treats, I won't be able to get you out of my head."

What did that mean? Was he making fun of her? She hardly knew. Except for some church functions and shopping in town, her social interactions had been limited. Olivia wiped her sweaty palms on her clothes, wishing she'd worn something besides a shapeless gray housedress. Something, that was, less Jane Eyre-ish for a change. She thought about shaking his hand but then changed her mind. "I was hired as an assistant and, well, sort of a nurse to your father."

"Sort of a nurse?" Noah released a chuckle. He knew he was being belligerent, but the moment was too much fun to let go of.

Olivia raised her chin a mite. "Some years ago Finney got a letter saying that you were dead." She smacked her hands together in a squirming knot.

"Dead? So I died? Well, that explains so much." He laughed. "Good to know."

"You laugh like your father."

"Oh? Is that right?"

The woman went into a quiet stare again. She didn't appear to be easy with banter. Her fingers now worked the pockets on her dress like little animals working at the locks on their cages.

Noah made himself at home, milling around the room. "Do you mind if I ask who sent the letter that pronounced me dead?"

"I'm sorry. I don't know."

Noah narrowed his eyes. "Whoever it was…was right." He stuffed his fists into the pockets of his jeans. "I guess I *have* been dead for years."

Olivia looked puzzled, as if she wanted to smile but couldn't quite get the muscles to obey.

Noah picked up a brass compass off a table and turned it around in his hand. "This was a gift from my father on my tenth birthday. He told me to be careful, or it would break. I treasured it. I really did. Never even used it, for fear it would be damaged. Even kept the outside polished. But it stopped working one day. I never did know what went wrong with it."

He tossed it in the air and then caught it in the palm of his hand. "I didn't take the compass with me. Too many memories attached to it…and not the kind you press into a scrapbook." Noah set the compass down, knowing he'd need to stop stalling and ask about seeing his father. "I'm here to talk to my father. I want to speak to him right now…even if he doesn't want to see me."

Her face went as ashen as her dress, which had to be the least flattering outfit he'd ever seen on a woman. And what was the meaning of that red ribbon around her wrist?

"Are you okay?" Noah reached out to her and cupped her elbow, thinking she might pass out.

"I'm fine. But Finney isn't fine. He's…" Olivia pushed

her long hair away from her face and then held that pose as if she wasn't sure what to do next.

"Please tell me, what's wrong?"

"Your father has gone."

"Gone where?"

Olivia grabbed her waist. Her delicate, elfinlike features wrinkled. "Your father has gone to heaven."

"He's dead?"

"Yes."

Lord, help me. I've come too late. "When did he die?"

"Three months ago."

Noah stepped backward and then collapsed onto a wicker chair. He'd been a fool to wait. Considering his father's advancing years, he should have known that the window of reconciliation would not stay open forever. Noah lowered his head and let his fingers claw into his scalp.

Olivia walked over to him and knelt beside him. "I'm so sorry. I shouldn't have just said it so bluntly. I'm not very good at—"

"What did my father die of?" Noah looked at her.

Olivia's soul wilted at the sight of Noah's eyes, which were now shadowed with grief. "The doctor said he died of heart failure. As I'm sure you know, he was seventy-six." Wanting to console him, she put her hand on his sleeve. "There is something else you should know, although it doesn't seem like the right time to—"

"What is it?" Noah broke their connection and squeezed the bridge of his nose with his fingers.

"I think you should know that, well, your father gave me the house. He left everything to me." But the truth was that if Finney had known his only son was alive, he never would have given her Bromfeld Manor and all his possessions. It had to be true. Then the next truth hit Olivia. She couldn't stay in the house. Not now. She could never take something that really belonged to someone else.

Noah's face took on a vacant stare as if his body were no longer aligned with his spirit. Then his gaze morphed into a glare. "You did well for yourself. Tell me, did you help my father? Did you...?"

"What do you mean?"

He drooped in his chair. "Maybe the doctor was wrong. Maybe you helped my father to heaven early so you could help yourself to his house," he hissed at her as his gaze pierced her through.

Shock over his words drew Olivia back on her heels. Tears pooled in her eyes, blurring her sight. "Surely you don't mean that. Finney was..." No need to say more.

Noah didn't appear to be able to hear her. He seemed to have drifted off into a place where she could no longer reach him. His face twisted in agony—a grieving that was beyond her own.

He reached out for the compass on the small table, and in the process his hand brushed against the pressed bluebonnet. Instead of picking up the compass, he placed the flower in his palm and slowly closed his fingers around it, crushing the wispy petals.

She felt Noah had crushed a part of her, as well— her spirit. *Oh, Lord. Please help this man.* In spite of his foul mood, she thought perhaps she should stay to help him just as she'd served his father. But since Noah believed she was capable of taking his father's life, he would want her out of the house immediately. It was time to pack her bags and go.

Olivia rose from the floor and tiptoed out of the room. How had her simple life gotten so heavy? It was as if she were carrying stones in every pocket. She trudged up the narrow curving staircase at the back of the house and made her way up to the attic room on the third floor, a room that had been her tiny abode for the past twenty years. Soon Bromfeld Manor would be just a lovely memory. Oh, well. It'd be the last time she'd have to listen to the squeaking fits of that silly ol' fifth step, but it would also be the last time to roam the woods she'd grown to love. Perhaps even the last time to know the joy of a real home. Mist stung her eyes. How foolish she'd been to think the dream could go on forever.

She pulled her two unused suitcases off the top shelf of her closet and filled them with all her possessions, marveling at how little she'd collected over the years. What she really owned—Finney would always say— were things of the heart.

Olivia closed up her suitcases and then searched the room. The only item left to take was a photo on the table. She picked up the frame and traced the two familiar faces, which weren't nearly as thin and plain as hers. It had been a childish idea, but since she had no family, she'd kept the original picture in the frame— the one displayed in the store. She'd never known the man and woman on the front, but they looked so sweet she didn't think they'd care if she imagined they were her parents. She'd given them names and histories and reasons—the noblest excuses, in fact—for their absence in her life. But most of all, she let herself believe they were both out there somewhere, loving her. Even though it was foolish, she couldn't stop herself from slipping the photo into her suitcase.

Olivia, you are such a mess.

Her gaze wandered to the canopy bed and the bookcase full of her favorite stories. This room had been a wonderful place—a cozy nook to call home.

Olivia closed the shutters, took one more sweeping glance over the room and crept back downstairs. The house felt anxious now, like the strains of an unresolved chord, but no matter how painful the situation had become, she wouldn't leave without checking on Noah.

She found him asleep at the kitchen table, with his head to the side, using his arms for a pillow. His fingers circled around an old harmonica, the one he must have been playing on the road. He appeared to have aged over the past half hour, or maybe she just hadn't noticed the lines around his eyes. The blood had dried up around the cut on his temple, but he would need to clean it up when he awakened. To make sure he was all right, she stayed by his side until she saw the gentle rise and fall of his shoulders. The poor guy was undone, but he would surely survive. At least he would have a home.

Olivia sat down on the chair next to him. "Noah, why in all those years…why didn't you come back, before it was too late? I wish we could start over, and we could just talk. I'd tell you how one of a kind and wise your father was. What a friend he had been to me. How he could quote poetry and compose music and make a room come to life with rainbows, simply by stringing broken pieces of glass together. I would've told you so many things. If only…"

Without thinking, Olivia reached out and touched Noah's head. His brown hair was loosed now and went in every direction like the feathers of some wild bird. The rose had fallen from his jacket. She picked it up to take in the scent and then slipped it into her pocket. She didn't want to wake him, so she prayed a blessing over him and rose. Just before she left, she took the ribbon off her wrist and draped it by his head. Olivia wasn't sure why she'd made such a gesture, but she wanted to leave that tiny token of herself behind. Maybe it was an exchange for the rose.

Then moments later, with suitcases in hand, she walked to the kitchen's side door. "Goodbye, Noah. I wish you well. I doubt I'll ever see you again."

When Olivia opened the door, Mops was there wagging his tail. She leaned down to scratch him behind his ears. The name Mops fit him well, since his scruffy hair looked like a raggedy mop. "Isn't that right, old boy?" But whatever went begging in his appearance was made up for in loyalty. "Take good care of Noah, won't you? You'll need to be brave, but don't go growling or nipping at him anymore, okay?"

Mops whimpered. "I've got to go, Mops. Please try to understand. I'm sorry I can't take you with me. At least not right now. But this is your home." The knowing and the loving were in the deep pools of his eyes and those eyes melted her, leaving her in tears. Olivia squatted down this time and gave Mops an old-fashioned hug.

Before Olivia could change her mind about leaving, she stepped into the garage, started the engine on her old Chevy and headed off down the lane. She switched on the radio and let it play anything it chose to, which was a woeful song by Loretta Lynn. How perfect.

Through the rearview mirror Olivia could see Mops following her, but soon he stopped and just stared at her. Even though he was too far away, she could imagine his eyes full of sadness. Such a faithful friend—old Mops. But in spite of the dog's lamenting gaze and her own breaking heart, somehow they both knew he needed to stay behind for Noah.

Olivia's old jalopy sputtered and coughed down the lane. The backfire—a ka-banging blast she never got used to—seemed like a noisy reminder of her less-than-stable future. She took in a deep breath. Maybe she needed some time to reflect on what to do next. Houston was only an hour or so away, but living in the big city didn't appeal to her. In fact, it seemed more than a little frightening.

She pulled over to the side of the road by one of the local fishing holes just outside of Gardenia. No one was there by the bank, so she parked the car, slipped on her sweater and then made her way to the water's edge.

The ripples caressed and teased the shore and lapped gently against the toes of her leather shoes. She backed away, not wanting to soil her only good pair of pumps. Still, it felt good to connect with something—anything—

even if it was the water from a muddy pool. On all her visits through the years she'd never once seen the bottom. She had no idea what creatures lurked just below the surface—beneath the film on top that reminded her of green skin. It was always hard to deal with things hidden—whether they came from a murky pond or life itself.

Olivia sat on a boulder to think of a way that she could navigate this dark maze she'd found herself wandering. *Oh, Lord, what can I do now?* A bird screeched above her with a lamenting call. She felt that same cry deep in her soul.

In spite of Noah's accusations, maybe she'd been too hasty in running off like that. The truth was, she had nowhere to go, no plan of any kind and no one to call on for assistance. She wasn't without church friends in Gardenia, but she didn't feel close enough to any of them to ask for help. She had no relatives to fall back on except an estranged uncle named Melvin, who hadn't even come to her rescue when she was a kid. It was unlikely he would help her now at almost forty. If that wasn't enough to fill the gloomy bucket, as Finney used to call it, she hadn't looked for a job in twenty years, and she had no real skills to speak of except for being someone's companion. Hmm. Small job. Even smaller life—almost as if she'd been sipping some Alice-in-Wonderland potion.

Olivia picked up a stone and tried skimming it on the pond's surface. Instead of silvery wrinkles, it made a kerplunk. A frog made a squeaking leap into the water next to her, startling her. Was the tiny beast frightened or celebrating his freedom?

She glanced up and spotted a narrow footpath through the thicket—one she'd never seen before. The rough trail reminded her of the walkway to the caretaker's cottage on Finney's estate. The old place was run-down but still livable. Maybe Noah would let her stay in the cottage until she could figure out what to do with her life. Besides, according to the will, she owned the cottage, the house and the seventy-five acres of meadows and creeks and woods—all of it. Of course, the will seemed like a joke with Noah's return. But surely he wouldn't throw her out into the street, especially if she offered to do some chores for her keep.

And there would be plenty of work, because Finney's inherited fortune had dwindled over the years and the estate had gone into disrepair. Maybe she could help Noah restore the house and the grounds to their former beauty. She had loved the manor. It was splendid with its gray stone and Gothic arches and peaks. A house straight from some fanciful tale. Hard to imagine that she, Olivia Lamington, had lived and worked in an English manor-style house. Perhaps, with some mercy from Finney's son, she'd be allowed to work there again.

Olivia rose with a bit of hope restored. Then she plopped back down. But if Noah did agree to her plan, she would be in his debt, which was a situation that gave her serious pause. She'd been vulnerable and needy before— with her foster mother—and that situation had turned dangerous and ugly and impossible to forget. *Oh, Lord, what can I do? Which way should I go?*

Chapter 2

Noah moaned from a place so deep inside he wasn't sure if he was awake or still in the midst of a dream. After a moment, he lifted his head from the table and glanced around. His mind blurred with such confusion he felt drugged. He rubbed his neck, which ached from sleeping at such an odd angle. For a second he barely knew where he was—or who he was—but then the place registered and the woman's words flooded back in an instant. The truth shattered his spirit once again like a sledgehammer on a plate-glass window.

My father is dead.

He'd come too late. Noah's stomach churned at the thought, and a bitter taste rose in his mouth. All the chances for reconciliation with his father were gone. Olivia had mentioned that his father had died of heart failure. It had crossed his mind in recent years that his father might have died over the twenty years of his absence, but he'd dismissed the concern, since his father had always been as hardy as the fig ivy that grew all over the manor. But now the hope of making things right with his father—to understand him, to talk through their past—would have to wait for their reunion in heaven. But by then, none of it would matter.

Suddenly clocks all over the house chimed and bonged and cuckooed. Noah had never liked clocks. They reminded him that life was always marching on and many times it was moving on without him.

He filled a glass with water from the tap and rinsed out his mouth. Then he milled around the downstairs, sipping water, still trying to wash away the awful taste of regret. He entered the living room, feeling lost.

He sauntered over to the fireplace mantel and picked up a random photo. The picture was of his father and Olivia, playing croquet of all things. They looked so happy, laughing as if they hadn't a care in the world. Why couldn't his father have shown him that kind of joy when he was growing up? The times they'd played catch, which were rare, his father had barely said a word. He'd made it seem that the time they'd spent together came from parental obligation—not from love. If Finney had been a real father, maybe Noah wouldn't have floundered in life, going from one job to another, never settling down or calling anyplace home.

And where were all their family photos? His fingers tightened around the frame as he placed the picture back on the mantel. Olivia. Humph. Pretty name—even pret-

tier woman. Noah certainly wasn't blind, but even with
her quaint charm and beauty and apparently the ability
to make his father laugh, he wasn't going to allow the
woman to keep the estate. He would have to hire an at-
torney to contest the will, to settle things properly. Although, at the moment, he didn't care about any of it.
For now, he felt like wallowing in his sorrow. Perhaps
he'd find a bed and sleep for a very long time.

Noah gulped down the last of the water and continued to stroll around the rooms, picking up knickknacks
and opening doors and studying his father's world. He
touched a palm frond on one of the potted plants. Hmm.
Artificial. The only thing he disliked more than clocks
were fake plants.

He glanced around at the stone walls and Gothic ar-
chitecture. What a big, empty beast of a house—cold
and useless and foreboding. Then with that last word—
foreboding—pieces of the past manifested themselves.
Sounds. Smells. Sensations of all kinds. Without warning, his mind flashed with images—scene after scene of
his life growing up in the house. Like smoke carried in
on a breeze, dark whispers accompanied the memories.

One of the murmurs seemed so loud, so real, he
jerked around, searching, thinking someone had entered
the room. "Olivia?" No answer. The horrific argument
he'd had with his father—the one that had made him
flee as a young man—surfaced with such force it became deafening in his head. He pressed his palms over
his face. *Not now, Lord. Please not yet.*

He called out, "Olivia!"

Except for the incessant ticking of clocks, the house

had an unyielding silence. Perhaps Olivia had gone outside to get away from him. Hard to blame her. Noah
berated himself for his heartless behavior toward her.
He'd been overtaken by her sudden news, and there
she'd been—a ready target. It had been too easy to un-
leash his misery on her. He remembered the compassion
on her face, even in the middle of his sinister accusations. Although there was also a time or two in their
conversation that Olivia's face had flushed pink with
indignation.

He touched his hair. Had he dreamed about Olivia
during his fitful nap? The images trickled back. Yes, he
had. The woman—who smelled like roses—had talked
softly to him about his father, and she'd even reached
over and rested her hand on his head. But why would
he dream such a thing?

Noah went to the small living room in the front of
the house and stood in the very spot where Olivia had
watched him walk up the lane. Absently, he lifted the
curtain and stared out the window. The last thing he was
in the mood for was company, but it appeared a car was
driving up the lane. As the vehicle got closer he could
tell it was Olivia. Had she fled the house without telling
him and then changed her mind? Or had she forgotten
something? Perhaps the furniture?

Noah opened the front door and stood on the front
step, waiting for Olivia to come to a stop on the circu-
lar drive. Her face—delicate and fair like the heroine
from a storybook—came into full view through the
windshield. Her head tilted as she gave him that distant stare again. Maybe this time he would find out

the "who" and the "why" of Olivia. With her unreadable expression, though, it was impossible to tell if the woman was poised for surrender or if this half woman, half cherub really had a quiver full of arrows hidden inside her bag. Whether the arrows were aimed at his heart or his inheritance, he couldn't tell.

Olivia had hoped to find Noah still in the kitchen asleep. Somehow it seemed easier that way. Maybe it made her feel less afraid, less intimidated. But there he was, awake and waiting for her at the front door. Had he seen her go? Maybe he wondered why she'd left so suddenly. But then anyone who accused an innocent woman of murder surely didn't expect to sit down a few minutes later and act as if nothing had happened. Finney, who'd been mostly warm and thoughtful in temperament, with few bursts of anger, apparently hadn't passed any of those fine traits on to Noah.

Now, Olivia. Noah has lost his father. His grief was acute. She would overlook his lapse in manners, as well as his cruel remarks. She opened the car door and went to stand in front of the first step that led up to the front door. She rested the toes of her leather shoes against the concrete step. "I came back."

"Yes, I see that." He grasped the iron railing.

Noah didn't invite her in, so she didn't move from the spot. "I left because…well, your father wouldn't have given me the estate if he'd known you were alive." She focused on the leather flowers on the tops of her pumps instead of his searching eyes. "I knew that right away.

In fact, I was about to tell you my thoughts on the matter when you…when you…"

"When I made my unforgivable accusation. I can't even repeat what I said. I don't know you at all. I don't know why I'd say such a thing to a stranger."

"Grief maybe?" Olivia looked up at him then. The blood on his cheek had dried, but he had yet to clean up the wound.

Noah glanced down the lane. "Yes, grief. And the shock of the news, although my father was getting up there in years. I should have…" His voice faded away.

"Life is full of those…should haves. They're as common as bees in the spring. I have some myself, from a long time ago." Olivia wasn't sure where her sage words had come from, but she wanted to at least offer him some comfort in spite of his earlier outburst.

"You're being generous. Don't let me off the hook so easily. I'm certainly not going to let myself off."

Olivia buttoned her sweater when a chilling breeze kicked up. "You're wrong about something."

"Oh? What is it?"

"You thought what you said to me earlier was unforgivable. But I do forgive you." She fingered the rose—his rose—that was still in the pocket of her dress. Perhaps later she would press it into the pages of a novel. Maybe *War and Peace* would be apropos.

"Thank you. Absolution is a good thing." He almost smiled. "I may need a lot more of that in the future."

"Future?" Perhaps Noah really would be open to the idea of her staying on in the caretaker's old cottage.

"Do you want to come in?" He opened the door wider. "Can we give it another try…if you'll let me?"

"Maybe." Noah's expression wasn't easy to decipher—maybe half bemused, half wary. Maybe it was the same look she wore. Olivia tried on a smile, since she didn't think it would hurt. "So, can you be trusted?"

"Probably not, but I still think we should talk." He made a sweeping gesture for her to enter.

Olivia hurried up the steps and breezed past Noah without glancing up at him. An unexpected rush flowed through her—almost as if she'd descended into a warm bubble bath. She wanted to blame her reaction on the balmy spring air, but she wasn't so naive to believe it. She'd flirted with the man—the same man who'd just insulted her earlier. What kind of a woman would do that? Apparently *she* would. *Olivia, you are such a child.*

"Do you mind if we talk in the kitchen?" he asked. "I haven't eaten today. Are you hungry?"

"No, I don't need anything. But I'd be happy to fix you a sandwich."

"I've become pretty self-sufficient over the years, but thanks." He pulled something out of his pocket—the scarlet ribbon—and offered it to her. "I believe this is yours."

"Yes, it is. Thank you." It felt silly now, leaving it behind. She accepted the ribbon and stuffed it into her pocket, hoping he wouldn't ask her about it.

"What's it for, if you don't mind me asking? You had it tied on your wrist earlier."

"Oh, it's what I call a 'memory ribbon' to help me remember things that are important."

"So, why did you take it off and leave it on the table next to me?"

Olivia looked at him. "I don't know. There was nothing left of me in the manor but memories, and I didn't like the idea of being forgotten completely." Was that too honest?

"I doubt anyone could forget you, Ms. Lamington." He motioned toward the kitchen. "Shall we?"

Minutes later, when they'd settled into the kitchen, Olivia stared out the back door. "Where's Mops?"

"Mops?" He paused in his rummaging in the fridge. "Oh. The dog."

"He's *your* dog now." Olivia opened a drawer and pulled out a first-aid kit.

"I have no idea where Mops went off to. Perhaps he found someone else to torture."

Olivia grinned and sat down at the table.

Noah stacked the fixings for a sandwich on the kitchen table.

"Mops is a good dog, really."

"He just doesn't like *me*."

"He'll grow to like you, I'm sure." Olivia opened the lid on the first-aid kit, pulled out an alcohol pad and tore it open. "Mops just needs some time to get to know your ways. He'll thrive on the littlest bit of love. Even just an occasional hug or a kind word. That's…" She stopped, amazed at herself for the way she was gibbering on like a goose.

"Yes?" Noah glanced up from his sandwich making. "You were saying?"

Olivia offered him the alcohol pad. "Your face. Don't you want to clean off the blood?"

"Sure." Noah reached for the pad, dabbed it on his temple and cheek and then tossed it in the trash. "Thanks."

Olivia opened a Band-Aid and motioned to him. "Why don't you let me put this on? It's so tender you might start bleeding again."

"Well, we can't have that." Noah leaned over and let her press the bandage over the wound.

She felt his breath on her hands, warm and tickly. "You don't look like Finney, but you do have some of his…mannerisms. Like the way you smile sort of lop-sided. And the way you swing your arms out with a touch of…bravado." She pulled away and wadded up the leftover strips.

Noah seemed to study her. "You did care about my father, didn't you? I can see that now."

"I loved him." Olivia's hand slid to her throat. "Oh, dear. That didn't come out right. I mean…well, not in the romantic sense. Not at all." She rearranged the condiments on the table. "There was no hanky-panky going on."

"Hanky-panky?" Noah licked the mustard off his finger and grinned. "I think that word went out in the eighteen hundreds."

Olivia frowned.

"Sorry. I'm being callous again. I do understand what you're trying to say."

"I loved Finney like a father. I never had one…not a real one."

"That I can relate to. In many ways I never had a dad, either, even though Finney was my father."

Since Noah's arrival he'd hinted at their unaffectionate relationship, but now the bold statement couldn't be ignored. "You must resent me. Now that you know how close I was to your father."

"No, not exactly resentment. But my life has been a puzzle, and now you're a part of that elaborate jigsaw."

Perhaps it wouldn't be so terrible to be a piece in someone's puzzle. It was a place to be, after all, even if it wasn't in someone's heart. "You make me sound mystifying. I'm really a vanilla-ice-cream kind of woman. No chocolate syrup or colorful sprinkles or anything that would make it special."

Noah gazed at her. "I doubt that. Everyone is special."

"Maybe." When Noah was finished building a ham sandwich, he said a small but stirring prayer over his tiny feast and dug in, eating quickly, barely waiting to chew.

Olivia broke the silence between them and said, "I'd like to help you, and since you're looking for pieces of your puzzle, if I were you…I'd start with the closet. Your father's closet."

"Oh?" Noah poured them both some iced tea. "Why there?"

"He wrote in his journal before he went to bed each night. He did this on and off for years, and he kept them in his closet. They're all neatly stacked in a row and all labeled. There's a good chance you can learn a lot more about who your father was through his writings." Olivia took a sip of her tea.

"You didn't read any of them?"

She set the glass down too quickly, making some of the tea splash onto the table. "No, of course not."

"I didn't mean to be insulting. But since my father died, I'm surprised that you weren't curious about what he'd written all those years. Perhaps it was about you. According to the will, you owned everything, so you had a right to look through the journals before you disposed of them."

Olivia wiped up the tea with a paper towel. "I would never throw them away. I just felt it was too soon to decide about his possessions, any of them, even his clothes. He was still too much a part of this house to let go of him…or the memory of him. I admit, a couple of times I stood staring at the journals, and I ran my fingers along the spines. But I never read them."

"You make them sound like sacred texts. I assure you, they're not. And my father is dead. His journals no longer matter to him…*wherever* he is."

"Wherever he is? How can you say that?" Olivia picked up the first-aid kit and put it away. "Your father loved Christ more than life. He's in heaven." She slammed the drawer shut with more fervor than she'd intended.

Noah paused, drinking his tea. "Don't get me wrong. That scenario is the worst of all human tragedies, but it's hard to imagine God allowing him into heaven after what he did to our family."

"I don't know what Finney did, but there is always the forgiveness of Christ."

"Yes, I'm aware of that. But…I'd better leave this subject alone for now." Noah reached for the harmonica, which still sat on the corner of the table.

What could she say? "Maybe it would help you to know that your father did grieve when he got the letter. The one that told of your death."

"Well, that's something at least." He ran his thumb along the mouthpiece. "But I'm going to find out who sent that letter." He squeezed the harmonica until it looked as though he was in pain. "Didn't my father question the letter? Where it came from? Whether it was a prank?"

"Yes, many times over the years. But I think the letter mentioned you'd died in some foreign country and you'd been…well, cremated there. He made some inquiries about it, but nothing came of it. You never came home, and there was no more information. So, eventually as each year went by, the letter seemed to hold more and more truth. He accepted it finally and believed you were, indeed, dead."

"Do you have that letter? Do you know where it is?"

"No, I'm sorry. I have no idea where it is."

"I see. Well, not really. But it's another piece of the puzzle, anyway." Noah pushed the other half of the sandwich away. "Look, as nice and decent as you seem to be, I'm still not ready to hand over my family's inheritance to you, but it sounds like we're in agreement that my return changes things, especially since my father really did think I was dead."

Olivia looked at the half sandwich on Noah's plate. Her stomach growled.

"I didn't come back to stir up any trouble," he said.

"What did you come back for, then? Really?"

Noah gestured toward the plate. "You look hungry after all. I don't want this other half. Please."

"Thanks." Olivia lifted the half sandwich from Noah's plate and took a bite.

"If you're thinking about giving me my family's estate back, I have to say that not many folks would be so compliant. Generally people would become embroiled in an ugly fight."

She pondered his words but didn't say anything.

"In spite of the way I came off earlier, I'm not really the kind of man who could toss someone out into the street. So, I have an idea…a proposal."

Olivia sat back slowly. "Okay."

"You obviously worked for my father for a long time, and I can see that he must have grown quite fond of you. I'm sure he'd still like to reward you for your faithful service. I'm not sure yet what that might be, but I do want to be fair. So, for now, do you mind living in the—"

"Yes?" Olivia leaned forward.

"You have a bit of mayo on your chin."

Olivia dabbed at the spot with her napkin but didn't take her eyes off Noah.

"I was going to say you could stay in the caretaker's cottage for as long as you need to, but suddenly it doesn't seem all that generous."

How wonderful. "But your plan is the same idea I

came up with. It was why I came back. Only I was going to offer to fix up the cottage as well as do some other chores as payment."

"That sounds like slave labor to me. You wouldn't be gaining much. Why don't we go have a look at this cottage before you commit to living there? That house is probably in a shambles after all these years."

"It's not fancy, but it's livable."

"We'll see." After a moment or two of silence, and she'd gone back to eating the sandwich, he said, "You seem thin. Didn't my father feed you?"

A bit of ham lodged in Olivia's throat as hard as an olive pit, so she took a few quick sips of tea. "I don't think men are supposed to say things like that to women they don't know."

"Sorry, I guess I can be too blunt."

"That's okay. Actually, I'm kind of out of practice when it comes to talking to...men."

Noah leaned back in his chair, looking at her. "My father was a man. You talked to him for twenty years. Sounds like you had lots of practice."

"Yes, but it wasn't the same." If she said any more on the subject she'd give away her thoughts. Noah was, after all, not an employer, but a man who was around her own age—and a man who was datable—even though such a thought probably gave Noah the hives. "In answer to your *other* question, I ate whatever I wanted to, but I was careful not to abuse his generosity. I knew your father's funds were dwindling. I was afraid he kept me employed out of loyalty. I wasn't sure he really needed me, although he always assured me he couldn't do without me."

"Hmm. So, where did you live all these years when you worked here?"

Olivia scooted her chair back, distancing herself from him. "The attic room on the third story. Why do you ask?"

"*That* tiny place? It isn't much more than the size of a closet."

Olivia flinched, feeling a little badgered. "It's cozy. I love it there. I didn't even move my things out of the attic after your father died."

"Really? That's amazing." He crossed his arms. "But once again, I see my father's negligence. There are plenty of big decorated bedrooms in this house. He could have offered you any of them."

Olivia tried to cross her arms, but her flustered state made her hands drop on her lap. She frowned.

Noah grinned.

"But I never needed anything bigger or fancier. It just wasn't necessary." At least that was what Olivia had always told herself. "I see where you're headed with this, but I can only say that your father was a good man. The best I've ever known."

"How many men have you known?"

Olivia wanted to give Noah a good slap, but when she realized he wasn't being cheeky, she said, "Not many, I admit. I've lived a pretty sheltered life in this house."

"It sounds like you've lived a trapped life, and for some reason you can't see it or admit it."

Olivia rose out of the chair. She wasn't going anywhere, but she couldn't stand to hear Noah's accusing words against a man who'd been her dearest friend. "I thought people weren't supposed to speak ill of the dead."

"That's just society telling us what to think. But the deeds of men, good or bad, are not buried with their bones, as Shakespeare might say. Their earthly actions live on inside other people. Their bloodied souls are still wrestling with those deeds...like me."

Olivia pondered his reply.

"I've offended you."

"I think you should be able to talk about this, but you have a tone. Your father was a fine Christian man. I knew him as long as you did, and he didn't seem capable of doing anything so wicked that his only son would abandon him for twenty years." Her voice built into such a loud fervor she startled herself.

"You have your story backward." Noah reached out to her, almost touching her hand. "By the way, are you always so bold?"

"Not really. No. You sort of bring it out in me," Olivia said. "You're like the squeeze on my tube of toothpaste."

A grin worked its way across his face. "But that's a good thing, right?"

"Not if the tube is on the floor and you're stepping on it."

Noah chuckled. Then he looked at her hand. "You're trembling."

Olivia placed her hands behind her back but replied, "So are you."

"Well, I was afraid you might run away again. Come on. Sit down. Please."

Olivia didn't budge.

"Okay. I'm sorry for my tone."

"All right. I guess." She eased back down on the seat again. "To be honest, you've got me all kerfuffled in my head. One minute you seem to be grieving over your father's death, and then you seemed to be consumed with anger."

"I feel some of both. I wanted to confront him as a man and not a boy. I wanted us to find peace, even though it seemed unlikely. But I knew God could do what I couldn't. And that was the hope I'd walked in here with early this morning."

"Okay. Why didn't you say that first thing?"

"Because I'm human and deeply flawed."

"Well, I can't argue with that."

Noah laughed.

Olivia couldn't help but chuckle. His laugh was contagious.

"Look, I can't lie to you or smooth it over. I won't. I did know another side to my father—I lived with it—and it was far from kindness. It must have been a side he never showed you. Why, I don't know. But it was his cruelty to my mother that drove me away."

"It's just so hard for me to believe." She shook her head, still trying to let the news soak in, but it was like rain running off a roof.

"So, you think I'm lying about my own father?"

"I don't know what to think." She kept her hands hidden since they were still quaking. If what Noah said was true, then she had believed a lie for twenty years. The man she'd respected and cherished—perhaps even idolized—was not who she thought he was. Had her sense of moral judgment been that critically flawed?

"So, you never saw my father lose his temper or suddenly act mean-spirited?"

Olivia thought for a moment, filtering through scene after scene when life had gotten tense. "He did get upset from time to time, but then doesn't everyone? And your father's occasional bouts of anger were usually righteous indignation. Even Jesus displayed that kind of outrage." Olivia studied him. "But you don't believe *me* now."

"It's obvious that you were very loyal to my father. I will try to respect that. But I think we're at an impasse… for now."

Noah's expression made Olivia wonder what he was looking for. Whatever it was, she wished she could help him find it.

Chapter 3

He looked down at what was left of her food. "Your sandwich has fallen to pieces. It doesn't look very appetizing. Would you like me to make you another?"

"I've lost my appetite." Olivia sighed. "Listen, I came off unkind just now, dismissing you and your feelings. I want to hear you out. I really would like to know why you left all those years ago. I want to know the details of what happened if you want to talk about it."

"Another time perhaps. Right now, I'd like to check out the cottage, you know, see if it's livable for you. And then I'm determined to spend the rest of the day snooping around this old house and reading my father's journals." Noah put the rest of the condiments away in the fridge. "So, I assume you'll want to go with me to the cottage."

"Yes, of course. Whenever you're ready."

Minutes later, Noah stared into the woods that had grown up behind the manor. "These trees. Amazing," he said to Olivia. "I should have expected this kind of growth over twenty years, but it's still a surprise to see this. Our gangly adolescent trees have grown into a mature woods. A real forest."

"I've enjoyed many an hour strolling through these woods. Sometimes I'd take a book and sit by the bayou to read."

Noah looked at her, grinning. "You were reading *Jane Eyre* no doubt."

Olivia looked at him incredulously. "How did you know?"

"Just a guess." Perhaps she'd read a bit too much of *Jane Eyre,* since her clothes looked like leftovers from a garage sale. But the paper-bag shape of her dress still couldn't hide her lovely figure.

"Please, go ahead." Noah gestured for Olivia to take the narrow stone path that led to the cottage. He wanted to be a gentleman to let her go first, and yet he admitted that he wanted to have a moment to observe her unnoticed. Olivia was a curious thing, and in spite of the odd circumstances they were ensnared in, she seemed more fascinating by the minute.

In the comfortable quiet between them, he watched her. Olivia wore not only vintage-type clothes but thin white socks that came to her ankles—the kind of socks schoolgirls wore back in the fifties. This curiosity was just another facet of Olivia's personality that gave her a waiflike charm and innocence. Olivia smiled, giving him a little wave, and then she gathered up a bouquet of Indian paintbrush and Mexican primrose. She stopped along the path to study the rhythmic drumming of a woodpecker and then the comical frolics of a squirrel circling around a tree. She obviously loved the natural world—as he did.

In between his study of Olivia, the woods couldn't help but capture his attention. The columns of trees, amid the carpet of ferns, had become all that he'd dreamed of as a boy—a forest of loblollies and live oaks and ash and maples—lofty and beautiful and proud. The local animals, the furry as well as the flighty kind, had come to set up housekeeping along with bugs and beetles. Oh, how he'd missed it, even the scent of the woods—the deep, earthy fragrance that made him believe he'd come across something otherworldly, something remarkable. The woods had been his first real playground as a child. Where he imagined his grand adventures and, most of all, where he first started to fall in love with his world of green.

Now, home again, he felt as if he could get a little lost in the woods of Bromfeld Manor. That was a pleasant thought, especially if he could get a little lost with Olivia, too.

In minutes they came to the stone cottage, which was situated in a small clearing. Noah stopped on the path and gave the building an overall assessment. "Hmm. I was afraid it might be in disrepair, but this is worse than I imagined."

"I think it looks enchanting, like something from a

fairy tale, especially with the vines growing over the stone and the arched wooden door."

"Enchanting? Hmm. Are you sure you're not thinking of Hansel and Gretel?"

"Nonsense. You just need to see the possibilities. I would love to live in this house."

Noah looked at the cottage again and then at her. "What do you see that I'm missing? With the mildewed stone, the broken shutters and the sagging eaves, it's a dilapidated mess."

"It just needs a little love. That's all."

"So, is love your answer for everything in this life?"

"Maybe. Shouldn't it be?"

"I wouldn't know. Love has been running from me ever since I was a kid." Noah turned his head this way and that. "Listen, I don't know if I feel too good about you living here until it's fixed up a bit. The inside must be a disaster. You could live in one of the bedrooms upstairs in the big house until we can make this cottage livable."

Olivia jerked in his direction as if he'd said an indecent word. "That wouldn't be appropriate."

"Well, then, you could stay in your attic room on the third floor. Far away from the dangers that are obviously lurking in the master bedroom on the first floor."

"I don't think it would be right. You're a man."

Noah laughed. "My father was a man, and you lived up there for twenty years."

"I think we've been through this before. I know he was a man, but he was—"

"I know. I know. He was old enough to be your father, and I'm young enough to be your husband. Right?"

Olivia hesitated in replying but, instead, marched the rest of the way up to the house with a back straight enough to make a librarian proud.

Noah grinned as he tried to keep his thoughts honorable about the intriguing Miss Lamington. Maybe she was right. Perhaps it really was inappropriate for Olivia to live and sleep under his roof. Too much temptation in those big brown eyes of hers. He was beginning to see why his father had enjoyed the woman's company. Why he'd kept her on even when he apparently could no longer afford extra staff.

Noah walked up to the front door. "So, who was my father's caretaker? I doubt that he was the same one I remember from all those years ago."

"His name was Samuel Klondike."

"Old Klondike?" Noah slapped his hand on the door. "I can't believe it. You can't forget a name like that. Or a man like that. And he must be about a hundred and fifty by now. I can't believe he stayed on so long. As I recall, he was always loyal to a fault, but also…"

"Eccentric?"

Noah chuckled. "To say the least."

"I was sorry that I had to let him go, but there just wasn't a lot of money left to keep a staff."

"No need to apologize. My father should have done a better job of managing the estate." Noah shaded his eyes and peered into one of the front windows. "The glass is so dirty I can't even see inside these windows." He turned to her. "I assume you brought the key?"

"Yes." Olivia pulled out a jangling ring of keys and handed it to Noah. "It's the skeleton one."

Noah looked at it. "Quaint." He slipped the ancient-looking key into the lock and turned. Something inside clicked, but when he gave the door a push it wouldn't budge. "What's that sound? It's outside." Noah stopped. "Is it growling?"

"It's Mops." Olivia backed away from the door. "The sound is coming from the east side of the cottage."

Noah left the key in the lock, and, with Olivia following close behind him, he took the footpath to the other side of the house. Just around the corner Mops stood snarling at something emerging from the woodpile—a rattlesnake. The beast slithered perilously close to the dog, and then the serpent's body coiled up like a spring while its tail rattled a fierce warning.

"Mops, stop that. Get away from there!" Olivia started after the dog.

Noah latched on to her arm, holding her back. Quickly he picked up a dead branch and, in one sweeping motion, scooped up the snake with the stick. The creature coiled around the limb but kept up its twisting, writhing rage. The snake struck at his hand but missed. Before the beast could strike again, Noah flung the serpent along with the stick into a nearby ravine.

He released a lungful of air, lowered his hands to his knees and tried to slow the boom-banging of his heart. Time and time again, a moment of joy would be subdued by a snake in the woodpile. And, in life, there always seemed to be a serpent waiting patiently in the wings.

Olivia rushed over to Mops, hugged him and said, "You silly pooch. You know better than to take on a rattler. You're too old for this nonsense." Then she turned to Noah with a frown. "And I could say the same thing to you."

"I'm too old, you mean?"

"No. You could have been bitten, and you could have died."

Her sudden ire surprised as well as amused him. Could it be she already cared about him a little? Noah refused to grin. He wanted to tell her that what he'd done was nothing, but her concern was too endearing to make light of.

"You're being too much of a hero." Olivia continued her blustery and adorable fuss.

No, my dear, that's not my problem. He was never much of anything—especially a hero. But Noah simply said, "I was careful, Olivia. I promise."

This time when Mops approached him he didn't growl, but instead gazed up at him as if he understood that Noah had given him something far better than a bone to chew on.

"Yes," Olivia said to Mops, "You'd better not snarl at Noah. He risked his life for you."

Noah lowered the back of his hand to the dog, and, after a second or two, Mops sniffed it and then licked it with slobbery gusto. "So, I guess that means we're friends now?"

"I think it does." Olivia smiled. "Thank you. Mops

gets himself into trouble from time to time, but that could have been serious."

"Well, I've gotten myself into scrapes over the years, too." He reached down and gave the dog a good scratch behind the ears.

Mops hunched down next to Noah's feet and rested his head on his shoes. "Well, how about it if you come with us to explore the cottage? Sounds a lot better than a bite on the nose, eh, boy?"

Mops raised his head to him, and if dogs could grin, he did.

The three of them traipsed back around to the front of the cottage, and Noah pushed on the door. "It probably swelled up in the spring rains." When it wouldn't dislodge, he gave the door some old-fashioned encouragement with a pounding bash from his shoulder. The door finally yielded to the blow, making Noah explode into the house and tumble onto the floor.

Olivia ran to him. "Are you okay?"

"Probably, but I think my shoulder didn't appreciate meeting this brick floor."

She offered her hand.

Taken off guard by the gesture, Noah gripped her hand and let her help him up. "Makes me feel like an old man, having you lift me like that."

"You shouldn't feel that way. That's just society telling us what to think." She gave him a sheepish grin.

So, Olivia really did know how to banter after all.

"Besides," she said, "you look like you have a little tread left on your tires."

Noah laughed.

Olivia blushed.

Cute. In their short time together, Noah already knew Olivia well enough to know that she'd embarrassed herself with her teasing.

She whirled into the tiny kitchen and began opening cabinets as if she were a detective in search of clues. Faithful Mops followed behind her into the kitchen.

Noah watched them puttering around together while he rubbed his throbbing shoulder. Then he turned his attention back to the living room. "This is not good. Tattered curtains that are too dirty to use for rags. Heaps of old junk." The place smelled dank too, along with the faint aroma of body odor and some other scent he didn't even want to think about. "Klondike loved the outdoors so much I think he brought most of it inside with him. You could plant a garden in here there's so much dirt."

Olivia popped her head up from underneath the kitchen counter. "Did you say something?"

"You surely don't want to stay here. It's a mess." He kicked the small couch, and dust rose in puffs. It was almost funny it looked so wretched. In between coughs, he said, "It will take a month's cleaning and repairs to get this place livable."

She brightened, waving a bottle of cleaning spray. "I just found a whole treasure trove of cleaning supplies under the kitchen sink."

"And I'm sure they're all unused. You know, for somebody who was caretaker, ol' Klondike certainly didn't take very good *care* of his own space."

Ignoring him, Olivia hurried off into the one and only bedroom. A few moments later she emerged with a stack of bedding. "At least all the sheets and blankets are washed and ready. That's good news."

Noah shook his head at her. So upbeat. The woman could probably spin straw into gold, too.

"Why are you looking at me like that?"

"You're being too long-suffering here. This isn't right. You should be upset or making some kind of demands. This place is a heap." He kicked at a pile of old magazines. "That's the most complimentary word I can think of. A heap. And it's a miserable heap at that."

"To me it's a challenge. It'll be fun to see how quickly I can clean it up and make it homey. It'll be a game... an amusement."

Amazing. Most women would think that a trip to Tiffany's would be an amusement, not endless hours of backbreaking work. "I'm not catching the vision with you, but I respect your need for a challenge. How about some help?"

"I don't think so." She tilted her head. "Nope. I can manage."

"All right, then. Clean away, but I'm right in the manor if you need me for anything. Heavy lifting or ladder stuff or a match to burn it down..." Noah stopped talking, since Olivia no longer appeared to be listening to him. Instead, she scurried around stacking the counter with liquid soap, paper towels and a big plastic bucket.

Time to go. Time to find his father's journals and learn more about the man who had been more of a mystery to him than a father. Noah took one more glance back at Olivia and Mops. The dog seemed to sense her

eagerness and bounded around her, barking with enthusiasm.

He would drop in on Olivia later to make sure she
wasn't overwhelmed with work, but, for now, he strolled
out of the cottage and headed back toward the big house.

On arriving at the back door, he turned toward the
side of the house, thinking he heard the snap of a twig or
saw a movement. Was someone lurking around, or had
the trees dipped and swayed in the gusts? There were
no fences to keep anyone out, but there never needed to
be. He'd felt it once before, since he'd arrived, a disturbing feeling—an awareness that he was being observed.
Bromfeld Manor had always seemed a bit creepy at
times because of its Gothic design, and when he was a
boy the house did get his imagination going a few times,
but the sensation he had now was more than a childhood fantasy. Nevertheless, he would let it go—for now.

Noah glanced up at the sky and the blue-black clouds
gliding their way. He could detect the smell of rain in
the air. Such a great scent, a promising scent. Thinking practically, though, he hoped the roof on the cottage didn't have a leak.

Once inside the house, Noah went straight to his father's bedroom. He paused just inside the doorway and
looked around. The king-size bed was made up with
a red-and-brown quilt and matching pillows. He wondered if that was where his father had died. Maybe it
was best for him not to know, though, since he intended
to make it his bedroom.

Noah opened the closet door and switched on the
light. The closet looked smaller than he remembered,

but probably because it was stacked high with boxes and clothes and miscellaneous stuff that people collected over decades of their lives. But there was no sign of his mother's clothes, just as there didn't appear to be any photos or any of her belongings left in other parts of the house. Apparently, all had been disposed of. It was almost as if she had never lived in the house—or ever lived at all. It was as if he'd only dreamed her up.

On one of the shelves was a long row of binders. Those had to be the journals. Out of curiosity concerning Olivia, he reached up to the volume that had her name printed on the spine. He lifted it down and opened it. Dust flew, making him sneeze. Obviously no one had read the diaries in years. He recognized his father's distinctive handwriting, and it was legible, but the entries were somewhat faded, the paper brittle and yellowed. He scooted down to the floor and rested against the wall of the closet as he read the first entry:

I see now that an absolute darling has come to work for me.

Her name is Olivia Lamington. She has been my aide for almost all of April, and already I can tell she is a treasure.

She is as kind and helpful as she is witty and intelligent. And, most importantly, Olivia has a rare gift that others do not possess—she sees life as I do—through the looking glass.

There was nothing more on the page. He flipped through, reading bits and pieces here and there. The journal did indeed appear to be all about Olivia, and his father's comments, which were long and detailed, always sang her praises. Noah turned to the back page, wondering if his father's opinion of Olivia had changed over the years. The last journal entry read:

My years are nearly spent. I am old, and yet Olivia keeps me humming along. She cares for me, assists me in all my creative endeavors and is faithful to a fault. Olivia, who began here as a member of the staff, is now a member of my family—and my most beloved friend. She is the child I longed for, the daughter I never had.

When Noah read the last line, pain pinched his heart like a rope on its final twist before it frayed. Why had his father not felt that same affection for him? Even as a child he'd sensed his father's indifference toward him. His strange detachment. What had he done to make his father dislike him so much? Had he been a bother and not a blessing?

Given his father's attitude toward him and the abominable way he'd treated his wife, perhaps Noah shouldn't have fled. He should have confronted his father in a more civilized manner rather than exploding in a rage and storming out for good. He should have stood up to him in resolute firmness but with love. Looking back, the act of running away had been the coward's way out.

Noah skimmed page after page, and he found his father's words to be nothing but glowing about Olivia. She really had served his father for twenty years. No doubt she'd been devoted and hardworking and loving. Noah knew it had to be true, since Olivia hadn't even tried to put up a fight for the estate. No one he knew would have given up so much so easily. And Noah discerned that Olivia's acquiescence didn't come from a subservient attitude but from a sense of moral rightness.

Noah rose from the floor and accepted the hard, cold fact that even if his father had known his only son hadn't died, he still would have willed everything to Olivia. What an unpleasant truth—a bitter pill. He slapped the journal shut.

He rested his head against the wall of the closet and rubbed his neck. A vicious headache was coming for a visit, perhaps for an extended stay.

One by one, his fingers closed, making a tight fist. Droplets of sweat trickled down his neck. Resentment was so real to him it became an ugly taste in his mouth. If he chose to let it stay—let the acid gnaw at his stomach and then his soul—there would be nothing left of him in the end. At least nothing worth salvaging. He knew himself well enough to know that disaster would be inevitable if he didn't do something. Now. Most people waited their whole lives, hoping to encounter that one defining moment—the one moment that showed they could become who they were meant to be. Perhaps they could become someone who could change the world or at least a piece of it. Well, he felt it all the way to his soul—this was that crucial moment—the one that might never come again.

A generosity of spirit was his only release from bitterness. His only flight to freedom. It would mean making a few things right. Big things. But then sometimes peace came at a high price. It wouldn't be the last stage to his cure, but it would be an epic beginning! Was he a buffoon? Probably. But he would be free.

Noah picked up the journal and slipped it back onto the shelf. He knew what he had to do. He would take Olivia out to dinner, and he would offer her back what she already legally owned. He would give her everything. Like turning the unexpected card over in a card trick, he would surprise her. As of tonight, they would trade places. She would once again become the heiress to Bromfeld Manor, and he would humbly request to stay in the caretaker's cottage.

Chapter 4

Olivia dragged yet another garbage bag full of junk out the back door. It clattered and banged all the way, until she gave it a whirling heave-ho into the outdoor pile. She lifted the top of her blouse and covered her nose and mouth. What a stench. She'd never seen so much worthless rubbish in her life. Had Samuel Klondike been a secret hoarder? It was true that some folks had a lot of secrets. She wondered what Noah's secrets were. She could tell by his demeanor and his occasional faraway gazes that his heart had a few to hide.

Thunder circled the cottage, rumbling around like a bunch of grumpy old men. The spring storm had yet to bring any rain, so Olivia opened all the windows and doors to let the fresh air blow through. It would help clear out some of the fusty smells. Then she headed to the kitchen and got busy cleaning it, since that room appeared to be the dirtiest spot in the house. What was it about men and their inability to take out the trash and do a bit of scrubbing? Everything, including the cabinets, counters and floor, had a thick coat of grime, but she was determined to see it all cleaned before the end of the day.

Even though Finney had employed a part-time house-keeper, Olivia had helped out with the cleaning when it was needed. She had learned at a very early age how to work hard without complaint. Of course, the way in which she'd learned her lessons had been at the malevolent hand of her foster mother, Mrs. Adder. She could still recall with clarity how the woman's hand, cold and pebbly as if it were made of bits of cobblestone, had squeezed her own hand until tears came—all because she hadn't made the bathroom sparkle to the older woman's liking. And if Olivia ever spoke up for herself, she'd be given time-out in the broom closet for the rest of the day. And night.

Those had been such lonely years, but she'd been jubilant to leave at eighteen and find a good place to live and work. In a way, Finney had saved her, given her a life, a home. Olivia stopped her scrubbing on the counter. What had Noah said? That she'd been trapped? She'd never looked at it that way before. But in truth, she had stayed so busy with Finney's many tasks and projects that she never did find time to go out and have fun with other people her age or take trips or date and marry and have a family. Looking back, perhaps she had given up a lot, but it hadn't seemed that way at the time.

Olivia rinsed out her begrimed washcloth with hot water, soaped it up again and went back to cleaning and chasing her trail of thoughts. It had indeed been so simple to use Bromfeld Manor as a refuge. Every time she left the house to run errands, she felt cloaked in—what was it—ordinariness? She felt awkward and bumbling socially. A total misfit. But when she came home to Finney, she felt once again transformed into a treasure that had just been found in some hidden vault. "Hmm. It might have been too easy, too pleasant here." She stopped for a moment and looked at the dog's gentle expression. "Maybe Noah is a little bit right, eh, Mops?"

"What was Noah right about?" a voice asked from behind her.

Olivia startled and dropped her rag. When she saw Noah, who was standing in the doorway, her face heated up like a tin roof in July. "Oh, I was just rambling on. Mops is a good listener."

Noah strolled through the open door. "Wow, it already looks better in here. What did you do with all the junk?"

"I put it in some beefy trash bags and dumped it out back."

"Good. Yes. Excellent." Noah seemed fresh out of words when he gazed at her. "It's about to rain."

"Rain?"

"Outside. The storm."

"Yes, of course, so it is." Olivia smiled. "Are you bored with the journals already? It looked like quite a collection of writings."

"No, not bored. *Enlightened* is a better word."

"Good."

Noah stopped in front of the kitchen counter, across from her. His hands were clasped behind his back, which gave him a smidgen of a schoolboy look. "Maybe it's a bit lonely in that house. Awfully big."

"Yes, it is." Olivia wanted to say that Finney's light always filled it up, but she didn't think it was the right time to praise his father. "Did you come to do some heavy lifting?"

"Yes, I guess you could say that. But first I'd like to take you out to dinner. If you want to go…with me. You know, for food."

Why was Noah suddenly so nervous? "Dinner?"

"Yeah, you know that thing people do when they get hungry."

"You're being silly." Olivia grinned. "But really? You mean eat dinner *out* with you?"

He nodded. "Maybe one of the nicer places in Gardenia."

"I would like that. Yes." Hopefully she hadn't jumped on the invitation too quickly. "I'm just not used to going out to eat." Ow. That came off as pathetic. But she was accustomed to having meals at the manor, since Finney saw no point in eating out.

"So, would you like to go with me?" Noah put his hands on the counter.

"You mean, go out like two friends?" *You're fishing, Olivia.* She'd probably broken some cardinal rule by asking Noah that question, but in spite of her ignorant queries, she wanted to know Noah's intentions.

"Well, yes…brand-new friends. But you could think of it as a date. If you choose to."

"A date. You and I would go on a date? Are you sure?" Olivia tensed on the rag, making the dirty water leak between her fingers.

"Yes. I'm sure." Noah laughed. "But I think this has been the longest day of my life."

"Are you too tired to go out? I could fix you something."

He leaned toward her and whispered, "Why are you trying to talk me out of it?"

"I'm not." Not at all. She glanced down at her scruffy clothes and the dirt under her fingernails. "But I'll need to change. And all my bags and things are still in the car."

"You may stay here, and I'll bring everything in."

"Really? All right." Olivia stared after him as he walked out. She bit her lip, barely able to contain her joy.

After a few minutes Noah came through the door with her two suitcases and set them down in the living room. "This is all you own—in these two bags?"

"It's all I ever needed."

He shook his head and smiled.

It was a smile she'd already seen a few times on Noah's face—the one that let her know she wasn't like other women. But she wanted to be. She just needed some practice. It was kind of late at nearly forty, but as Finney used to say about age and dreams—one was never too old to try. Olivia raised her chin and said in a more exalted tone, "You may place my bags in the bedroom."

Noah grinned.

Olivia laughed at herself. Oh, dear. Those dark eyes of his, luminous and probing—how would she ever survive the evening? She sighed, but in her heart, so he couldn't know. Who was she to be? Just being herself on a date would surely be a disaster. It always had been before.

Noah took her bags into the bedroom and then returned. "I'll leave you to it, then, but I'll be back in thirty minutes."

"Yes." Although it would take a lot longer than that to look presentable.

Noah headed out the open door, still smiling.

It was so good to see him smile. The long day, which had started so grievous and confusing and lonely, might still end with some measure of joy.

She ran into the bedroom, threw open her two suitcases and dug out all of her dresses like Mops might do tunneling for a bone. She would wear her prettiest dress—the blue one with the flared skirt. When she found it on the bottom, Olivia held it in the air and waved it like a flag, feeling like Cinderella going to the ball. She danced around in little circles with abandon, full of more excitement than she could remember. She even broke out into song with "Olivia has a daa-ate. She has a ree-eal date. And she's going to wear panty hose and scandalous red lipstick." In the midst of her merry jig, she glanced up.

Noah stood leaning against the door frame, watching her and grinning wider than a cat spying a mouse.

Olivia collapsed on the bare mattress, mortified he'd seen her foolish parade. Why hadn't she shut and locked the door?

"Sorry," Noah said with maddening calmness, "I forgot to ask if you like seafood."

Olivia sat there for a moment, and when she could finally find her voice, she asked, "You mean you still want to take me out…after that?" Her chin quivered.

Noah went to Olivia's side. "May I sit down?"

"Yes, of course," she muttered. "Why do you ask?"

"Well, this is a bed, and I am a man, after all."

A tear wet her cheek. "Are you making fun of me?"

"No, no. I promise I'm not. That was so insensitive of me. I wanted to make you laugh, but my timing was off." As usual. "I'm sorry." Noah eased down next to her. He wanted to put his arms around her, but they hadn't known each other long enough for him to be so intimate. So, he sat there like a lump—hoping she wouldn't flee from his oafish ways.

"I'm such a ninny."

"You are not. That moment just now was free and honest. And girlish."

Olivia snorted out a laugh. "You mean childish."

Noah pulled back and really looked at her. "I mean girlish, and I say that as a compliment."

"But I've no right to be girlish. I'm going on forty." Olivia wadded up the blue dress in her hands.

"I'm going on forty, as well."

She sighed. "But you're a *man*."

"So you keep telling me."

Olivia brightened a little. "You have that twinkle."

"I know. I work on it in the mirror when you're not around."

She grinned.

Okay, making headway. Noah gently peeled from her hands the blue dress, which she was still strangling, set it on the bed and smoothed out the wrinkles.

"Thank you." She swiped a single tear away and straightened her shoulders.

What had he been thinking, standing there with as much sensitivity as a clod of dirt? He should have backed away when he saw Olivia's little dance, knowing perfectly well it was meant to be a private moment. But he'd witnessed a rare treat—the world of an innocent—and he couldn't help but enjoy the moment and want to see more. "This has been an extraordinary day, hasn't it? Full of sorrow. Blame. Revelation. Forgiveness… surprise."

"I've never had a day like it before."

"If you think you're too worn-out from it all, we can go out to eat tomorrow."

Olivia ran her fingernails along her bottom lip. "No, that's okay. We'd better go this evening. I mean, you might change your mind by tomorrow."

Noah laughed.

"Am I being funny?"

"You're being…enchanting." Just what his father must have thought of her. In fact, he thought his father would have married Olivia had he been younger.

"I promise I won't change my mind, but let's go out this evening. I was looking forward to seeing you in this blue dress *and* with your scandalous red lipstick. And I'm not teasing you. I mean it. I promise." In fact, it scared him a little just how much he meant it. "And too, I have something important I need to tell you, but I'm certainly not going to do it while we're sitting on this filthy mattress. I cringe to think what's living inside this thing."

Olivia ran her hand along the ribbing of the mattress. "It'll be more comfortable than sleeping in a closet."

"A closet?"

"It's where I used to sleep some. I was an orphan, and I grew up in a foster home." She hated the word *orphan*. It was such a hapless, almost sullied, word, but it was a word she'd gotten used to hearing at school. She could so easily recall the whispers, especially on parents' day, when no one came to the school to support her, celebrate her—love her.

"That sounds much worse than my youth. In fact, it sounds like someone needed a few years of jail time."

"Probably, but I guess I never thought of it that way. Funny, the unnatural things people grow to accept when there's no one to tell them otherwise. I guess I learned early that life is no bed of roses."

Yes, but he had the power to make life easier for her. "Tonight, at the restaurant, I would be honored if you want to tell me more about your childhood."

"My tale of woe?"

"Yes."

"I might tell you some of it." Olivia lifted her dress off the bed. "I guess you'd better let me get ready."

Noah rose. "I shall return." He left the room, and, this time, he shut the bedroom door like a gentleman.

After a shower, the first thing she did was ditch the little white ankle socks in favor of a real pair of panty hose. As much as they were a torture to wear, a woman couldn't feel fully dressed up without them.

An hour later they sat eating salmon and wild rice in The Royal Gardenia Café, although he couldn't find anything royal about it. Noah glanced around and leaned over the table toward Olivia. "Sorry, the salmon chews like jerky. You may throw out your jaw gnawing on the stuff."

"It's not too bad. You just have to pour more of that lemon-butter sauce on it."

With an exaggerated gesture, Noah poured out the last of his white sauce on his slab of fish. "I guess Gardenia, Texas, was never known for its gourmet fare."

"I don't mind. It's amazing to eat fish again of any kind."

"You don't eat fish? It's good for you."

"Finney, that is, Mr. Bromfeld, didn't like fish, so it was never ordered for dinner."

"You may call my father by his first name," Noah said. "Surely you did while he was alive."

"I did. But I suddenly felt strange saying it to you just now. Don't know why."

"By the way, why didn't my father like fish? What's not to like about it?"

Olivia paused and looked at him as if she didn't want to say more on the subject. Then she blurted out, "He had something like a phobia concerning fish, especially eating them."

Noah washed down another chunk of salmon with a gulp of iced tea. "My father had a fear of fish? I never knew. I've heard of all kinds of phobias, but never that one." He tapped his fork on the salmon, and it actually bounced. "Maybe my father had eaten one too many fish dinners in Gardenia."

Olivia laughed.

Noah loved to hear her laugh. It had sort of a bur-bling brook, almost musical, quality to it, but he also noticed that when she chuckled she covered her mouth with her hand in a shy, endearing manner. After a re-flective pause, he said, "I wondered how many other oddities Olivia had to endure to make life with my fa-ther bearable. Simply because, once again, no one was keeping watch over her."

Olivia went quiet.

Perhaps he'd offended her. Again. He wondered about his clumsy attempts at romance. Was that what he was doing? Romancing Olivia?

"I do admit something."

"Yes?"

"Your father was…unconventional."

"Yes, to say the least."

"But I always thought of it as charming." She smiled and added, "Actually, he had a lot of funny sayings."

"Like what?"

"Well, when everything was going his way, Finney used to say it was a paint-the-house-purple kind of day."

"And what does that mean?"

"It just meant it was one of those rare days when it felt like you could do nothing wrong. That even if you painted your house purple, you wouldn't regret it. You couldn't, because it was your day in the sun." Olivia gave a one-shoulder shrug. "I guess saying it out loud now, well, it seems kind of silly, but I always thought it was a quaint and amusing thing to say."

Noah wasn't sure what to make of his father's idiosyncrasies, but he did love watching Olivia talk about them.

She pushed what was left of her salmon to the side of the plate and took another bite of rice. Perhaps she'd given up on the main course, too.

"You look wonderful in that blue dress, by the way."

"You've said it three times, but that's okay. I love hearing it." Olivia grinned. "I bought it secondhand at a used shop, but it's made well. It'll get a lot of wear. Don't you think?"

"I do." Noah winced in his spirit. The thought that Olivia still had to pinch pennies, probably because his father paid her a poor salary, irritated him. Considering her childhood abuse, he could hardly think of it. But no more. There was something he could do about it. "Remember, earlier at the cottage, I mentioned I had something to tell you."

"Yes." She opened some more sugar packets and poured them in her tea. "What is it?"

"As you know, I read some entries in one of my father's

journals. The first one I opened started with you, and it ended with you. I read enough of it to know how he felt."

"Oh?"

"He grew to care very much for you. In fact, he loved you like a daughter. You had been right about everything. Except for one thing. He would not have changed his mind about the will had I come home before his death. I know now that he wanted you to have everything, and I have decided to honor that request."

"What do you mean?"

Noah placed his napkin on the table. "I mean that I'm officially giving you back the estate. All of it. No other papers need to be written up or signed, since you legally own it anyway. But I wanted you to know that I won't be fighting the will."

Surprise lit Olivia's face like the sun coming up on a cloudless morning. And her lips, which formed the little O, appeared so sweet he stared at them. "You're welcome to say something." Guess she was in shock. Noah had things he wanted to ask her and things he wanted to tell her, but for the moment all he could think about was how much fun it would be to kiss those ruby-red lips.

Chapter 5

Olivia dropped her teaspoon. Then she shifted in her chair. She had assumed Noah would offer her a small gift of money from the estate to thank her for her years of service, but never had she imagined that he had changed his mind completely—that he would want her to have everything. He couldn't do it. She wouldn't let him. "My answer is… I mean it has to be…no."

Noah nearly choked on his rice. He drank some water. "But you can't say no."

"I think I already did." Olivia twisted the napkin in her lap. "I don't mean to come off ungrateful. I am very touched by the gesture, moved by your generosity. You see, I live so frugally that what's left in the estate moneywise would have lasted me the rest of my life. So, what I'm trying to say is…it's no small thing what you're doing by making me that offer, and it's no small thing that I'm giving it up. But I still cannot accept it."

"Why?"

"It just doesn't feel right owning everything now that you've come home. If I became the beneficiary now, and I offered you the cottage, it would bother me every single morning that I rose in my bed in the big house while Finney's son was rising in the caretaker's cottage or some apartment somewhere. No matter how fond your father was of me, you are his only son. You are the true heir to Bromfeld Manor."

Noah threw his head back, laughing.

A man and woman nestled in a corner booth glanced over at them.

Olivia was startled at his outburst. "And what is so funny?" She frowned, studying him. "I can't see one funny thing here."

"If people could hear us, no one would believe it. *I* can't even believe it. Two people arguing, trying to give each other a large estate, and neither one willing to take it."

"Yes, I guess that is sort of funny. If I did agree, which I'm not, what would you do for money? Didn't you say on the way over here that you were out of work?"

The waitress swooped over to refill their iced teas, eyeballed their lack of interest in the fish, shook her head and then left again.

When she left, Noah said, "Yes. I did lose my job in Dallas. That's true. But I moved to Houston recently with a plan. Over these past twentysomething years I've lived here and there, and I've had some odd jobs, good ones and bad ones. I even worked on a cruise ship for a while, but none of those paths led me toward what I wanted to do. My ultimate goal is to start my own land-scaping company. I've taken some horticulture classes, and some in business and landscape design. I think I'm ready. That's the plan, anyway."

"Really? So, you love trees and flowers? Like I do."

"Always have." Noah twiddled the white daisies in the vase.

Olivia looked at his hands, tanned and sturdy. She could see him working the earth, making it grow all kinds of wonderful things. "Ralph Waldo Emerson said, 'Earth laughs in flowers.'"

"I've always loved that quote."

They stared at each other for a moment, basking in what appeared to be mutual admiration and affection. His look became so warm she glanced away before she could blush to the roots of her hair. "I think your idea of starting a landscape company is a good one, but it would take a lot of cash—capital, I guess they call it—to start a company like that. What's left of your father's money would be the answer. It could help get you started."

"Olivia, you're thinking I'm poor. I'm not rich, but I do have some money saved."

"Well, you *did* show up at the house with no car."

"Yes, true. I guess I did show up looking like a gypsy." Noah grinned. "It's a long story, but a friend of mine dropped me off this morning. I own a pickup, but it's in the repair shop. And I do have money saved from a few real-estate deals. So, I'll be all right."

"So, does that mean you'd start your landscape business in Houston?"

This time, Noah squirmed in his chair. "Maybe."

"You know, this area is growing. Some of the people at church said it was from all the retirees wanting to move out here from Houston. They want to move somewhere quieter with a bit of land and some pretty trees. So, maybe there'll be a greater demand for new homes and…landscaping." She hoped it wasn't too obvious that she was trying to get Noah to stay, but that was exactly what she hoped to do.

"Are you actually trying to get me to stay in the Gardenia area? Could it be that you like me a little?" Noah slapped his hand over his heart.

Olivia looked away, trying to keep her composure. "Well, yes, but I was also thinking from a job-related angle, too. If you start up the business, that's just the sort of thing I would enjoy." She always was better with plants than people.

The waitress toddled over, pulled her glasses down on her nose and rubbernecked back and forth, gaping at their plates. "My mama, who's tenderly called Miss Jewels, always says that folks should clean their plates or at least pretend to. Mmm-hmm."

"Well, it's a good thing your mama isn't here, then, isn't it?" Noah grinned.

The waitress wagged a finger at them. "I'm thinking you both don't like the food. You two just keep smearing it around the plate hoping it'll disappear all on its own."

"Maybe we could use some more of that lemon-butter sauce," Olivia suggested.

"That a girl. Now we're talking." She picked up the saltshakers and made them do a little jig on the table. "You got it. Oh, yeah." The woman did a fast duck-waddle back to the kitchen.

Noah looked in her wake. "Memorable waitress."

Olivia chuckled and dug into her asparagus, hoping to please the faithful daughter of Miss Jewels and hoping Noah would forget the direction their conversation had taken.

Noah slid his hand over to hers but didn't touch her. "You're not getting off that easily. You didn't answer my question."

"Yes, I like you a little. But if you persist, I'll have to keep reminding myself why I like you."

"Do I detect a *tone?*" Noah reared back, looking wounded.

"Maybe."

He smiled. "I have an idea. Let's compromise. I'm going to be blunt now, so brace yourself."

"All right." She wasn't sure whether to be happy or scared.

"In spite of the *unusual* circumstances we've found ourselves in today, we seem to like each other. I enjoy your company, and I can barely remember the last time I could say that about a woman. I've found many of them to be manipulative and selfish. Sorry to be so down on your sex, but that's been the bulk of my experience. So, my idea would give us time to explore a friendship, maybe more. I could stay in the cottage, and you could stay in the manor. But—"

"But I think—"

Noah put up his finger to silence her. "Now, now. I agree that nothing is set in stone. Okay? This is a fluid agreement. So…we can fix up the house and the cottage together as time permits. I'm not tied to a job right now, and I can give up my apartment in Houston easily enough. While I'm staying at the cottage I could check out the area to see if there really is enough potential business for a landscape company here, and you'll have a place to stay as long as you need it or want it. Win-win, as they say. So, how does that sound?"

Olivia paused, thinking of each angle of his proposal. "Your plan…hmm. To be honest, a spaghetti strainer has fewer holes. But…"

"But?"

"Okay, for now, it'll do." She reached out to shake his hand. "You have a deal, Mr. Bromfeld."

"Good." Noah shook her hand but held it for a moment longer than he needed to.

What was she getting herself into? Perhaps something lovely, something she'd waited her whole life for and didn't even know it. It was so hard to know the ending of a story on the first chapter.

"Just out of curiosity, after my father died, didn't you get lonely in the house? Or scared, all by yourself?"

"It was an adjustment, but I'd been there for so long that I was glad to stay on. Glad for a home but, yes, it was different being by myself in such a huge house. Lots of echoes and memories."

"When I was a kid I used to think the house talked to me. You know, all those moans and creaks. I imag-

ined that it had a personality of its own beyond whoever merely lived there."

"Wow, I wasn't scared before, but I think I am now."

"Oh, no." Noah chuckled. "I'm sorry. I didn't mean
to do that."

"It's okay. I guess I'm not as fragile as I look if I can
stay in that house by myself."

"I think you're like one of the live oaks around the
estate, sturdy and steadfast and well rooted."

"So, was that a compliment?" It was hard to tell,
since it made her feel as pretty as a tree trunk.

"Okay, okay. Let me try again. If you know anything
about balsa trees, you know that the wood is amazingly
delicate looking…but incredibly strong. Is that better?"

"It'll do." She smiled. Oh, yes, she would tuck that
compliment away for future use when she felt particu-
larly vulnerable.

"Good," he said. "By the way, sometime soon, I'd
like to take you somewhere."

"Oh?"

Noah picked around on his plate. "Well, you asked
me why I fled from Bromfeld Manor twenty-odd years
ago, and you deserve an answer…all of it."

"So, where are you taking me?" She looked at him
with renewed interest.

"I'll be taking you to the cemetery."

A few days later Noah found himself at the cemetery
with Olivia. He had no idea what the town's cemetery
would look like after so many years. He hadn't visited
his mother's grave in two decades, but he was glad

that on his return visit a woman named Olivia Lamington was by his side. He opened the wrought-iron gate that led to the graveyard. It released a harsh and grating squeak as if it were some disapproving gatekeeper. "Thanks," he said, "for coming with me today."

"You're welcome. I assume we're here to visit your parents' grave sites?"

"Yes. I'm pretty sure their plots are over by that old oak tree." He pointed to the only tree in the cemetery.

"Yes, that's where we buried Finney." Olivia clasped her hands together behind her back, which seemed to be her habit when she was anxious about something.

Noah motioned for her to go ahead of him on the well-worn path through the grass. "Did my father visit this place through the years?" He'd hesitated to ask Olivia the question, since he was worried that her answer might put him in a stormy mood.

Olivia cleared her throat but didn't reply.

"Please tell me that he visited at least once or twice over the years."

"Oh dear, oh dear," she whispered. "I wish I could lie to you to make it easier. But I can't."

"No, I want the truth." No matter how painful.

Olivia stopped and turned to face him. "I don't think that he ever visited here. Anytime he wanted to go somewhere, I always drove him, so if he'd chosen to come here, I would have known."

Noah shook his head and plodded on ahead of her. What could he say? It wasn't her fault, and yet he felt like hollering at someone. Anyone who would listen.

When he came to his parents' graves near the oak

tree, he stopped. Instead of flowers, prickly vines grew on top of his mother's grave and almost covered over her name, which was etched on the stone marker. His father's grave was still fresh with its mound of dirt, but even it appeared despoiled with weeds. The wind whistled through the headstones, making a mournful sound. What a cheerless place. "So overgrown," he murmured to Olivia when she quietly stepped beside him.

"I'm sorry that I didn't keep them up. Before Finney died, I never came out here, but then when he was buried…well, the times I came to visit made me so desperately sad that I stopped after the first few weeks."

"It wasn't your job to tend my parents' graves. It was mine." Noah reached down, wiped away the vines on his mother's granite memorial and read the words engraved there. "'Here lies Evelyn May Bromfeld.' I remember my father had wanted something simple, but it's so plain it's…it says nothing of her life."

Olivia touched the sleeve of his sweater. "What happened to your mom? You told me she was struck by lightning, but you didn't say how she died."

"The lightning didn't kill her. I have my father to thank for that."

"What do you mean?" Olivia's voice was gentle and searching.

Even after only a couple of days of getting to know Olivia, she already seemed like a friend, a good one— so maybe it would be best to finally lay his burden down. It was time to tell his story. "The lightning incident caused my mother to have some eye damage. But she also suffered from vertigo and confusion at times.

The doctor couldn't guarantee how fast she would recover, and my father didn't deal with the changes very well. My parents never did have a close relationship, but this put an even greater strain on their lives. My father became impatient and belligerent when she got confused over things. It was heartbreaking, seeing her try so hard. Watching their lives unravel until there was nothing left."

Olivia hugged her waist.

Noah looked up at the sun, which had hidden behind the clouds as if it too were saddened by his story. "It's turning cooler." He looked at her, took off his sweater and placed it around her shoulders.

"But I don't want *you* to be cold."

"My anger will keep me warm." He stuffed his hands in the pockets of his jeans. "In answer to your question, my father refused to deal with the changes in my mother, even though I think most couples would have been able to handle them just fine. Some days my mother was back to normal, so I knew she was improving and healing. But my father somehow convinced her that she was losing her mind and that she needed to go to a mental-health facility in the city."

"Oh, my." She pulled the sweater more closely around her. "Did your mother go?"

"Yes, but she only lasted six months in that place. The doctors said she died from sleep apnea, but I know she died of a broken heart. My father had abandoned her. When she was alive, I went to see her as often as I could, but with each visit I could see she was losing hope that she'd ever be able to come back home. I encouraged her to move into an apartment. At least she'd be free of that awful institution. That prison. But then one day my father took a phone call, and they said she'd died. I felt numb with grief. Her death had been so unnecessary."

"That is such a sad story. I'm so sorry. I never knew this. Finney never mentioned it, and I never thought it was my place to pry into his past." Olivia put her hand on Noah's shoulder. "When did you leave your father?"

"I wish I could say I just left, but I'm afraid there was a lot more to it than that. The day of the funeral, when we got home, I lost my temper. As a teenager I had quite a hot head, and that didn't help matters. But I went into a rage and called my father a murderer. Needless to say, it didn't go over well, and so I threatened to leave for good. When he sat in the chair as if he didn't care whether I stayed or left, I followed through on my promise. I left, and I never came back…until yesterday."

A little sob escaped Olivia's lips, and a tear trailed down her cheek.

"I didn't mean to make you cry." He offered her his handkerchief, and she dabbed at her face. "But I did want you to hear my mother's side of the story. I wanted you to know. It was important to me."

"It was a shock to hear it…more so than you can imagine."

When Olivia looked at him, her eyes were filled with understanding and transparency—an irresistible combination to him.

"I do believe you. I'm so sorry you didn't feel loved by your father growing up. And then to have your mother taken away like that. It was thoughtless of your father. I admit it. No, more than that. It was cruel of him."

"There's been no family to talk to over the years, and I've only mentioned it once, to another woman, and that one time I wish I hadn't said anything."

"I'm glad you felt safe with me. That you would trust me enough, even though we're only just getting to know each other."

A lone raven landed on his father's grave, and he shooed the beast away. Even though the ravens had fed Elijah in Bible times, he'd never liked the look of them. They always seemed to be curiously disturbing creatures, skulking about and gaping at people as if they were not only looking for something sinister inside a person but finding it. "I have to be honest. Some part of me wanted to protect you from the truth, since you loved my father. But another part of me wanted the relief that comes from having someone believe me, understand me. But I suppose it was as unkind as it was freeing. I know my story hurt you."

Olivia joined him by his father's grave. "It wasn't easy to hear. In fact, I'll never be able to think of Finney in the same way. It…it would be impossible to go back. Maybe it was just a dream world I lived in. To protect myself."

"You're an easy target. I get the feeling you've been that way your whole life." Though Olivia's eyes were full of compassion for him, they were also furrowed with confusion and pain. In spite of her devotion to his father, she'd chosen to comfort him, the path of kindness—putting his needs before hers—but it was obvious now that his story had wounded her. She seemed to fumble over her words as she tried to cope with his news. Perhaps his confession—his selfish need for freedom—had stolen the only joy she'd known in her life. Maybe he should have told someone else. His old pastor friend, Avery Martin, would have listened. Would have advised him. Too late now. Too late for so many things. "Maybe bringing things out in the open now is as helpful as returning a borrowed book to a demolished library."

"No, I'll be all right." She reached down and pulled a large dandelion weed from Finney's grave. "I'm glad you told me. I don't want to live in ignorance…in shadows."

"Do you see why I left all those years ago?"

"I do." She tossed the weed aside. "But I still wonder why you didn't come home sooner. Twenty years is a very long time."

"With each year it became easier to stay away. My father made no attempt to find me, so I assumed nothing had changed. One year became two and three and then decades drifted by. Life goes so fast, like a lightning strike, and unfortunately I know something about that act of nature." Noah knelt down and began pulling the rest of the weeds from his father's grave. "I lost my job and moved to Houston, then one morning I woke up and realized that someday it would be too late to confront my father, man-to-man. I suddenly wanted to work through the past, my anger. It would have been rough, but I thought it was necessary. It was time. But, as you know well, I was too late."

"I'm so sorry you didn't get that chance." Olivia knelt on the other side of Finney's grave and helped Noah make the small space a little more presentable. "I'm sure he would have wanted to see you. To talk to you. And I'm hoping he would have asked you to forgive him. I do know that when the letter came, the one that wrote of your death, your father was full of sorrow. He didn't seem to want to talk about it, though, so I let it go. But I wish I had questioned him more now. For your sake."

"It's all right. The last thing I want to do now is cast more blame on you." Noah rose and wiped the dirt off on his jeans.

The cloud of bewilderment in Olivia's expression morphed into fear as he helped her off her knees.

"What is it?"

"But how could I have been so wrong about another human being? Someone I'd known for so long? We shared hundreds of conversations. No, thousands. It not only frightens me to think of Finney this way, but it makes me question my own judgment, my lack of discernment, that I couldn't see he was capable of such cruelty."

"I will give you this," Noah said. "Perhaps my father thought about what he'd done to my mother. Perhaps there was some regret, and he'd made his peace with God about it. If that were the case, then he would have wanted to move on. Maybe he felt forgiven and didn't see any reason to tell you about what happened."

Olivia dusted off her denim dress. "That's very generous of you, to give your father the benefit of the doubt. But if Finney really had made his peace with God over what he did, then it seems to me it would have been easier for him to discuss it, not the other way around."

"I think we're both trying to find some middle ground here…in this dance of words."

"Have we found it?" She brightened. "Middle ground?"

"Maybe." Noah turned back to his mother's grave and read her name again. He remembered the stories she'd read to him as a child. The many endearing things she'd done as he grew up. She'd even taken him fishing since Finney wasn't interested. She'd been forced to be mother and father. What a burden for her, and what a loss for him. "I'm going to spend a little time cleaning up my mother's grave."

"May I help?"

"If you'd like."

They both knelt down and worked for a while, pulling weeds and vines from the grave site. It felt good to be digging in the soil again. Working odd jobs here and there, he'd forgotten how much he'd missed working with the earth—the smell of it, the feel and hope of it. When the small area was cleaned up, he said, "That looks better."

"Noah?"

"Hmm?"

"Do you intend to read some more of your father's journals?"

"Yes. Right after we get back. I had to take a break since I wanted to check out the house and the grounds. And work on the cottage. That's why you haven't seen much of me these last couple of days. But now after being here by their grave sites, I'd like to get back to it. Those journals are bound to have some answers. Maybe those entries will help me to close some doors once and for all."

"Well, would you mind if I read them with you? Would that be okay?"

Noah rose, helped Olivia up, but this time he held her a bit longer. She looked so vulnerable, so in need of some comforting, and yet he'd been the one who'd hurt her. Finally, he said, "Of course. I would be happy for you to read them."

As they walked back through the cemetery, they both fell quiet. The air was thick with the aromas of spring, which helped to lift his spirits. And too, there was a natural high in having Olivia so near him. Her long brown hair had been let down, and it floated and lit around her face in the breeze. Lovely.

He hadn't kissed her the night of their date. After settling Olivia back in the house, he'd headed off to the cottage for the night, berating himself. And yet the timing felt way off for more than a brief hug. He didn't think she'd trusted him enough at the time, and why should she—they'd only just met. And maybe he'd hesitated in kissing Olivia for other reasons. When he kissed her, really kissed her, there would surely be more change to come. In spite of his vacillation on the matter, he blurted out, "There's a place not far from here that I'd like to show you. We can walk if you'd like."

"All right. The sun's back out, and I think it might be a pretty day after all." Olivia slipped the sweater off her shoulders and handed it back to him.

They strolled along a new path now, until they came

to the edge of the cemetery, where no one had been buried because of a bayou. They walked across a footbridge
over to the other side and then stood beneath the wide
and welcoming boughs of a live oak. A wooden swing
suspended by ropes drifted in the breeze along with
the long tresses of Spanish moss. It was an irresistible
spot for a little romance. "I can't believe that old swing
is still here." Noah pushed on it and tested the ropes.
Seemed sturdy enough. "Someone must have replaced
it over the years."

"This place is lovely." Olivia sat down, and, without
saying more, he began to swing her. She laughed when
he pushed her extra high. Her effervescent laugh made
him laugh, as well. He would surely benefit from more
of that good medicine, especially if he could laugh his
life away with someone wonderful like Olivia. When he
brought the swing to a halt, he took her hand to make
sure she was steady on her feet.

Once connected, though, he didn't want to let her go,
and he could sense there was more going on between
them than friendship.

She didn't look all that anxious to release him, either,
so he held on to her hand. Indeed, the moment had arrived. He glanced upward at the sky and the swirling
clouds. This would be their moment. He would make
sure of it.

Noah moved closer to Olivia. Even without the lipstick, her lips looked full of delight—like finding a
ripe strawberry hidden among the leaves. The desire to
partake of that sweetness went from inviting to urgent.

Perhaps sensing that he would kiss her, Olivia's eyelids fluttered shut as she tilted her chin upward. There was something so endearing about her gesture that he paused, looking at her face, taking in all the soft lines and curves. All of it seemed lovely to him—the oval shape, the lush brows, the tiny freckle by her mouth, the dimple on her chin, even the spray of lines at the corners of her eyes. Apparently, she was just as full of expectation as he was, and he had no intention of disappointing her. He cupped her face in his hands, leaned down to her and brushed his lips against hers.

Chapter 6

At thirty-nine—Olivia had finally experienced her first kiss. Would she hyperventilate from the excitement? Or giggle like a dizzy teenager? She'd seen enough romantic movies to know how it was done, so maybe she should try to make the most of it. Such a blessed event might never come again. She slipped one hand around the nape of Noah's neck and fingered his hair. Oh, how she loved touching his hair, even from that first day. Imagine Olivia Lamington kissing a man with long hair. Noah was such an exotic man for such a plain girl. She stretched her other arm across his back and drew him closer. *Oh, my.* Noah certainly responded well to her gestures.

When the grand and giddy, exquisitely tormenting

event was complete, they eased apart. But they still gaped at each other, eyes wide.

Olivia clasped her hands behind her back. "Are you breathing?"

Noah laughed. "I'm not sure. Maybe you'd better check."

She grinned.

"You look a little flushed yourself," Noah said.

"I am blushed. I mean flushed." In fact, being rosy from a kiss was pretty wonderful stuff. No wonder men and women loved it so. It was a fine earthly endeavor. A pleasurable pursuit of great magnitude. Far better than any craft project or board game. A real kiss felt like a marvel, especially when it was shared with someone like Noah. "Is it okay to kiss like that in a cemetery?"

"I don't think we're going to get much opposition. Do you?"

Olivia shook her head but grinned.

He ran his finger along her cheek. "I've wanted to kiss you ever since I stepped into the sunroom and saw you with that broom aimed at my heart."

Olivia laughed, covering her mouth. "I've wanted to kiss you ever since I touched your hair while you were sleeping in the kitchen. I shouldn't have, I know, but I couldn't seem to help myself."

"Sleeping in the kitchen? Oh, you mean when I'd sort of passed out on the kitchen table." Noah rubbed his chin. "Really? So, that wasn't a dream after all. It was you."

"It was too forward of me. Too intimate, since we'd just met."

"It was…unforgettable." Noah sat down on the swing as if to ponder her confession.

Perhaps it said too much about her. It probably did, but, for once, Olivia didn't care if someone could see inside that quiet place in her heart where no one else had gone before.

Within her own private moment, she could see with clarity now how odd it was that she'd kissed the man who'd just given her the sinister news about Finney, the news that her longtime employer wasn't the charming older gentleman she'd thought he was. The fact that she could secret away such a revelation in the back of her mind, so she could fully enjoy Noah's kiss, seemed a little bit beyond the pale, as her favorite Gothic novels would call it. Was that how other people did it? How Finney had pulled off his secret life? He'd found hiding places so deep in his spirit that he could forget about the lifelong pain he had caused?

Olivia took the silky breeze into her lungs and let it revive her. She would choose the higher road and give Finney the benefit of the doubt. She would hold on to the hope—even if it was only by a thread—that Finney had deeply regretted what he'd done to his family and had moved on in his knowledge that God had forgiven him for his sins—all his sins. Perhaps she should forgive Finney, as well, and move on. But how could she forget the suffering Finney had caused Noah? The lost years between father and son? Not to mention the emotional havoc it had brought his wife and the way it altered their family forever with her death.

"You're thinking about my father, aren't you?" Noah was staring at her now.

Olivia jostled herself out of her daydream. "Sorry, I got lost there for a minute." She nodded. "Yes. I was thinking about Finney. How could you tell?"

"It's the same frozen gaze I must have when I'm thinking about the past."

"Oh." Olivia tried to animate her features to encourage Noah.

Noah pointed to her wrist. "I notice you're wearing the red ribbon. What are you trying to remember?"

Olivia thought for a moment and said, "I forget."

They burst out laughing.

After a moment, Olivia said, "Maybe this is a good time for us to search those journals. Find more pieces to the puzzle. Because once a puzzle is put together and looked at, it's much easier to put it away on the shelf. Don't you think?"

"So, are you going to say that sage advice came from my father?" Noah asked.

"No. I read it in a book." She lifted her face to the sun, letting it warm her skin like a sheet right out of the dryer. What a day with such unhappiness and joy, but then the clear and murky waters of life usually ran in the same stream.

Olivia looked to her side, thinking she saw something stirring in the cemetery. It was probably just another visitor, but when she studied the spot where she'd seen the movement, no one was there. Lately, she'd gotten the feeling that she was being followed. Studied. Surely it was her imagination, but it felt unsettling.

She didn't want to alarm Noah unnecessarily, so she said nothing to him about it as he escorted her from the cemetery.

When they were at the big house and settled at the kitchen table with a pile of Finney's journals, Olivia asked, "Are you sure this is okay? For me to read these entries? I feel that I'm prying into your life. Maybe you should read them first, in case there's something here you wouldn't want me to know about."

Noah splayed his hands on the table. "I'm not like my father. I have nothing to hide." He released his breath all in one puff. "Please. Take one." He gestured to the top of the pile. "Be my guest."

"All right." Olivia took one of the leather-bound journals off the top of the stack and cracked it open. Papers fell out and fluttered to the floor. They looked down at what had fallen out of the journal.

Noah picked up the papers and stared at them. "Oh, my. My father must have forgotten he'd put these in here."

"What is it?"

"They're stock certificates. With seals." He flipped through them. "They're real. I wonder why he didn't put them in the bank."

"I didn't mention this before, but as he got older, Finney did get a little forgetful."

"Well, that's understandable at his age. But what a shame if these had gotten lost or thrown away by accident." Noah shook his head.

"Are they that valuable?"

"I'll have to make a phone call to someone who knows more about stocks than I do, but yes, if these oil-company stocks went up as much as I think they did over the past few years, they're quite valuable." He shook the wad of papers in the air and let out a whoop. "This really is an amazing find. It would be a great help to…us. Perhaps this would be enough to hire contractors to refurbish the house and cottage, bring the estate up to its former glory quickly. If you and I try to do it ourselves, it would take several years—especially if we can't devote all our time to it."

Olivia wouldn't admit it to Noah, but it didn't sound like a hardship to her that the house and cottage would force them together for years to come.

"When I first arrived, the house didn't look all that run-down, but the more I've looked around the house and property, the more I've noticed all kinds of problems. This place needs lots of repairs. Things my father neglected over the years." Noah shook the stocks and then laid them before her. "This could be the answer."

"That's very good news." Olivia glanced over the documents. She'd never seen a stock certificate before and had no idea what they looked like, but these certainly looked official. "Would you like a mug of coffee to celebrate?"

"I would. But I'm making it. You've served this family enough."

"If you insist."

"I do."

"Well, then, I like mine with a little cream, no sugar." Olivia opened the journal again and began to read, but after the first paragraph, she stopped. Her fingers trembled as they lit against the words, words that were intensely personal.

Noah glanced over to her from his work at the counter. "What's wrong?"

"I just wasn't expecting anything so direct…about me." Did she really want to reveal Finney's thoughts when they were about such a personal issue? But then Noah was certain to read the entry sometime anyway. "I might as well read it to you. Finney writes…

"Olivia would heal if only she could confront her foster mother, Mrs. Adder. When I hear her weeping, it nearly stops my heart.

I know the secret of why she refused the refurbished bedroom on the second floor. She likes the smallness—the confinement—of the attic room. It reminds her of the broom closet growing up.

This tiny space of her youth was, of course, a place of punishment, but it was also a place away from that hateful woman's verbal abuse. A quiet place, a sanctuary."

Noah put down the coffee grounds and stood across from Olivia. "So, my father did offer you a better place to stay in the house after all?"

Olivia strained to bring up the past conversations on the matter, but no memory of his offer came back to her. It had vanished like morning fog. "It was so long ago I just don't remember. I suppose Finney's comment would explain why even after he died I never moved from the attic into a larger bedroom. I could have. I heard someone once say that prisoners have similar troubles, you know. They can't seem to handle the wide-open spaces of the world when all they've known is a prison cell. They want to go back to what is familiar."

"Do you want to talk about it? About Mrs. Adder?"

"I don't know. I've never really talked to anyone about it except Finney. It's pretty depressing. I doubt you'd want to hear it."

Noah sat down next to her. "Why wouldn't I?"

"These aren't pleasant things."

"And I suppose my stories have only been about tea parties and Sunday-school picnics."

Olivia grinned. "I guess you're right. My story is like yours. An unhappy childhood."

He gave her hand a squeeze. "But I knew the love of a mother, and I wasn't forced to stay in the broom closet."

"Well, I only had to go there when I was bad."

"You? Bad?" Noah said. "I'm trying to imagine that."

"Well, I guess I should say…I had to go to the broom closet when Mrs. Adder said I was bad, which was most of the time. The woman was mean-spirited and miserly. She would have made Scrooge look generous. And she had a thing about judgment."

"Wow, sounds pretty scary."

"To a little kid it was. I often thought that Mrs. Adder was like the oleander flowers that grew in our neighborhood. She'd be all perfumey and sweet when caseworkers came around, but it was only pretend. The moment the front door was shut, she was back to being poisonous…just like the plant." Olivia tried to chuckle. "Maybe her attitude would scare me even today."

"How did you make it through?"

"The mercy of God."

"Why didn't you tell someone about the abuse?"

Olivia fingered the embroidered violet on her dress. "I got the idea that if I went somewhere else…to another home, it would only be worse. Of course, that kernel of fear was planted there by Mrs. Adder, and that seed grew well and stayed green all those years growing up. Then, when I was nearly grown, I knew I would be leaving soon, and so I felt I could put up with her meanness awhile longer. And by then I'd gotten used to her ways and I'd learned better how to avoid confrontations with her. Then, when I turned eighteen, I found your father's ad in the paper. Maybe now you can see why Finney's attention and kindness to me was so deeply appreciated."

"Yes, I see. I do," Noah said. "So, you don't remember your real home? Your mom and dad?"

"Not really. I was told by the caseworker that they'd both died."

"So, what do you think about my father's idea? Of finally getting some closure with Mrs. Adder?" Noah rested his hand on the back of her chair.

"You mean going to see Mrs. Adder? Actually talking to her?"

"Well, yeah, that's what I mean. I will take you if you'd like. And you'll be able to face her as a grown woman. You'll be able to do what I couldn't do with my father." Noah's voice was firm but also steeped in compassion.

"I've thought about it through the years, but I've never been brave enough."

"Then let me go with you. Between the two of us we'll have enough courage to confront the old battle-ax."

Olivia chuckled. "She'll give you the boot with those words, or she'll call the police."

"Good." His palm slapped the table. "And when the authorities arrive, we can report her abuse."

She shook her head. "You make it sound so easy."

"Well, of course. Advice always flows more freely when it's not your own life you're meddling with."

"True." She raised an eyebrow at him.

"We could go tomorrow."

"Tomorrow? That's way too soon." She gave her head a quick shake. "I need some time to think about it. Lots more time. Don't you think?"

"But you've had decades to think about it."

"Yes, but at least give me an extra day or two to practice what I might say."

"Of course, if that brings you some comfort."

"But no matter how much I practice my speech, facing Mrs. Adder will be as easy as walking across a bridge with no planks."

"I'll be right by your side." Noah put his hand up as if he was giving an oath. "And I promise to be the perfect gentleman while I'm there. I won't say anything to Mrs. Adder...unless I'm provoked."

"Well, that might be in the first five minutes."

Noah lowered his hand and rested it on her shoulder. "But I'm glad you'll get your chance before it's too late."

"It might already be too late. She may have died ages ago."

"And then maybe not." Noah gave her shoulder a squeeze. "I mean, aren't you curious? What if the hound of heaven got hold of her soul? What if she's a changed woman, and she's been wanting to ask you for forgiveness as she breathes her last breath?"

"Won't it be a waste of gas driving into Houston?" Olivia asked, thinking she was running out of excuses.

Noah held up the wad of stocks. "I think we can handle a tank of gas."

"All right. Okay. You've convinced me. We can try. I think I still know how to get to her old house, although I'll be surprised if she still lives there."

Olivia gave him her best smile, but inside she shivered. He had no idea what he was asking her to do. It would be one of the hardest things she'd ever done. Revisiting those terrible memories was like going down into a dungeon full of monsters. That hateful and mean woman. The harsh judgments and mistreatment. The house. The ache of loneliness it had given her. The longing for a mother and father, for love and hugs and laughter around the dinner table. All the things other children took for granted. But maybe with God's help and Noah by her side she could face it all. Perhaps Finney had been right about Mrs. Adder—Olivia wouldn't fully heal until she'd talked to her. Until she faced her as a grown woman.

Noah went back to the counter to finish making the coffee.

On a happier note, Olivia asked, "I have an idea. Since you're doing this wonderful thing for me, I will make dinner tonight, and you can be my guest. That way, you'll have time to read your father's journals."

Noah stared at her, shaking his head. "You are too good, Olivia. Women like you have to be careful."

"Careful of what?"

"Of men wanting to bask in the warm glow of your goodness."

"Is that what you think Finney did?"

"Maybe." Noah flipped on the coffeemaker. "But I guess I never really knew my father. Not well enough to answer your question with certainty."

Guess she hadn't known Finney, either—even after being with him for twenty years. If Noah had even a little of his father's deceiving nature, couldn't he turn out to be more of a danger to her than a benefactor? Perhaps she was in peril, and she didn't even know it. The former housekeeper at Bromfeld Manor, Lucile Barnes, had always told her that she was way too gullible for her own good. Maybe she was, but Olivia would let her concerns about Noah go—for a little while.

Chapter 7

An hour later, when Olivia and Noah had finished their celebratory coffee, Noah settled into his father's study with another journal while Olivia started on what she hoped would be an edible supper. That was the one thing Finney had rarely needed her to do—make dinner. He had always hired a cook, until Olivia let the woman go after Finney's death. Since then, Olivia had cooked for herself—but only the most simple fare, such as sandwiches or scrambled eggs.

So when Olivia pulled out a whole raw chicken from the freezer, she wasn't exactly sure what to do with it. After some thought, she stuffed the bulky beast into the microwave and hit Defrost. That should get the ball rolling. She was passing the window on the way to the pantry to retrieve a cookbook when something caught her eye outside on the back lawn. Some movement out of the corner of her eye. Was it Noah? She doubted it. He was most likely in his father's study. Had to have been Mops. Yes, that was it. But hadn't the shifting shadow been taller than Mops? Tall enough to be a person? Could it be the same person she'd seen at the cemetery?

Her concern was interrupted by a funny smell. Was it the chicken? Oh, no. She opened the microwave door. Melted plastic. How foolish. She'd forgotten to take the silly bird out of its package.

Where had her mind been? Probably on the attractive man in the other room. But the question now was: How was she ever going to make anything edible? She got out a cookbook and went to work.

What felt like hours later, Olivia put the finishing touches on a meal—what looked and smelled like a real meal, anyway. Maybe she should have put out the good china in the big dining room. No, the kitchen felt more casual, cozier. Noah would surely like that better. But just to set a softer mood, she lit the two candles on the table. Hmm. Not quite enough. She rummaged around in some drawers and found a dozen or so used candles, placed them around the room and lit them all. Nice. Now to find Noah. She guessed that he'd gotten wrapped up in his father's words and had forgotten about the time.

Olivia hurried to Finney's study to tell Noah the food was ready, but when she peeked around the corner, he wasn't there. Okay, maybe he was going through the many rooms of the house, or he'd gone for a walk.

"Yoo-hoo. Supper's ready." Her words echoed through the house.

Nothing.

In case Noah had gone exploring upstairs, Olivia went to the base of the staircase and called up to him.

The faint response, "I'm up here," reached her. Not wanting the food to get cold but also not wanting to raise her voice to a scream, Olivia headed up the curving stairs in pursuit of Noah and his appetite.

She gripped the railing, suddenly thinking of Noah as a boy, chasing around the hallways and up and down the big stairs. He must have had such fun, imagining that he lived in a castle with a thousand nooks and crannies to hide in. And it was more than a little delightful to know that over the two decades of living in the house, she'd walked all the places he'd walked. Gazed through the same windowpanes. Explored the same woods. Enjoyed the same vast library. Oh, how she enjoyed pondering all things Noah.

Hmm. Back to the matter at hand—feeding Noah supper. Maybe he'd gone to his old bedroom. She hurried down the hallway to the last room on the left. The door had been left ajar, so she gently pushed on it. The door squeaked the rest of the way open.

Noah stood by the window, looking out toward the woods.

Something was wrong, or he would have turned to her when she opened the door. "Noah?"

"Yeah?"

"I thought you might be in your old boyhood room."

"I'm surprised you even know which one it was.

Surprised Finney even told you. There's nothing left of mine here. Not even a photo. All given away or thrown away. Apparently Finney had a need to remove any trace of me...any memory. And now I know why. At least an awful lot of questions have their answers today. The last puzzle piece has been put into place today, and it makes a very ugly family picture."

"What is it?"

He still didn't turn to her but placed his palm on the glass.

"Noah?"

He pointed to one of Finney's journals, which lay open on the bed.

"So, there must be something in there that is...revealing?"

Noah exploded with a laugh. "Yeah, you could say that."

"May I help?" Olivia asked softly. "Please let me."

"You're welcome to read it. You might want to start with the words 'My wife could never be trusted. She and that boy of hers were cut from the same cloth.' He calls me 'that boy' as if I'm a stranger in the house."

Olivia walked over to the journal. "I'm so sorry." Maybe she shouldn't have encouraged Noah to read Finney's writings. Maybe it was a terrible mistake.

"His words do answer a lifetime of questions, though."

"Oh?"

"I know now why I never looked like my father."

"Why is that?" Olivia wiped the perspiration from her hands.

Noah looked at her, his face eerily bare of expression. "I don't look like Finney because Finney is not my father."

The truth crackled the air like the ill-fated lightning strike he'd heard as a young man. Noah didn't want to believe what he'd read in the journal, but he knew in his soul it was true. Finally the answers had come—the whys of Finney's aloof behavior all those years when Noah was growing up. Why Noah wasn't treated as a beloved son but an inconvenience, a nuisance. Yes, the truth would most likely set him free—eventually— but right now it felt as good as running headlong into a barbed-wire fence. He glanced over at Olivia, who appeared bleak with despair.

"This must be so painful." Olivia walked over to him and held out her arms.

He reached for her and took solace in her embrace. Her rhythmic breathing against his chest felt comforting, so he stood still for a while, gazing out the window.

Songbirds piped up, chirping and trilling on a branch near the window, belying the somber mood inside the house, inside his heart. Olivia seemed to wait for him to speak.

"As I said, Finney's not my father, but I'll never know who my real father is because, according to the journal, my mother was notoriously unfaithful in her marriage. So much so, that *she* never knew who my father was. I can't imagine that about her. That she could live such a double life. It would be a little like looking at your own reflection, only to see someone else. That would rattle anyone to his soul." He ran his finger along his forehead, wishing he could wipe away the lines and the years. "I suppose Finney could be lying, but there would be no reason for him to do so in his personal journal. He wouldn't lie to himself. How sickly funny. In the end, there were *two* people in this house who were playing masquerades."

Olivia rested her head on his shoulder. "I'm very sorry, Noah."

"I thought my mother was so saintly. So good. I still have this vision of her, playing old hymns on the piano in her Sunday blue dress. She taught me to play the piano…a little. And she taught me how to ride a bike, since Finney wasn't interested in teaching me. My mother had this gift of creating a safe haven with her love, but just outside that shelter were Finney's disapproving glares. Now I know why. I always thought my mother's trips into Houston were for shopping. I was so naive. But Finney knew the truth…that my mother was far from being a saint. Maybe that's why she went to the mental institution so readily. When I went to visit her she always talked as if she were guilt-ridden about something. Like she deserved to be there, to be punished. I never understood it. Why she would say such things. But I know now."

Olivia eased away from him. "So, does this change the way you feel about your father?"

Noah thought for a moment, at the various angles of the query. "Yes…a little. But Finney should have found a way to love a child who was innocent. I suppose he had Biblical grounds for divorce, but I wish they could have worked it out. As a kid you just want your parents to be happy so you can live your life. So you have permission to be happy. Or something like that. I guess grown kids want the same thing, though." He stared down at the trees. "There's a good view of the woods from up here, and yet you can't really see all the life that goes on inside the forest. I guess that's the way I knew my parents…from a distance."

"Maybe you wish now you'd never come back," Olivia said in a faraway voice. "I wouldn't blame you if you felt that way."

"No, I can't say that." Noah pulled her a little closer. "If I'd never come back…I wouldn't have met you."

Olivia smiled up at him, and it felt brighter than the sun streaming through the window. "I made you dinner, but I understand if you're not hungry."

"I don't know. I was hungry for the truth earlier, and look where that got me."

She seemed to search his face as if waiting for a sign of lightness in him.

Noah grinned. "Yes, let's eat."

"Okay."

He followed her downstairs. "What did you make? Something smells good."

"I made fattening food."

She sounded so excited to have someone's approval he wouldn't rain on her joy. "I've always thought the best food had to be fattening."

When they were seated in the kitchen on opposite sides of the table and had said a brief blessing, Olivia waited for him to take a bite before she dug in.

When he tasted the mashed potatoes, he nodded. "Okay. Now we're talking. Good and smooth. No lumps."

Olivia's shoulders relaxed. "I'm so glad. I wasn't sure how it would turn out, since, well, the chicken and I had a bumpy start earlier."

"You and I had a bumpy start too, and that turned out well."

"How true."

No matter how foul his mood, it was impossible not to notice how Olivia's face glowed in the candlelight. Maybe she hoped he'd chat some more. Since he didn't want her smile to fade, he said, "By the way, the candles are a nice touch. Unexpected. Appreciated. Lovely."

"Thanks." She cleared her throat, paused and then said, "You know, I understand if you don't want to go with me to see Mrs. Adder. I know this was such a blow that—"

"No, of course I'll go with you. I would never let you face that woman alone. Unless this is about you changing your mind."

"No, I haven't changed my mind." Olivia stared at her food and frowned. "But without you I wouldn't have the courage to go and see her." She took the saltshaker and gave her food a good coating of the seasoning.

"You have more courage than you think, Olivia Lamington. You had the courage to come back and face me, even though I'd proved myself to be a jerk."

"You're not a—"

"Yes, I was. A royal one. And I don't want you to think I'm comparing my situation to yours. At least I had parents who stayed with me. I was never banished to a closet. And even though my mother proved to be unfaithful to Finney, she at least showed me acceptance and affection. I have those things. Those memories. I know you would have felt blessed to have had a fraction of that love."

"Yes, but to grow up in a home where you desperately wanted and needed to connect with your father but weren't allowed to…is also pretty sad. And so unnecessary."

Right then Noah's heart filled with thankfulness for Olivia. What a treasure she was. Why hadn't some man snatched her up, married her? But then he didn't know all there was to know about Olivia yet, and one hard lesson they'd learned since yesterday—since the enlightenments—was that people were not always what they appeared to be. Even the family members they thought they knew as well as their own heartbeats had the ability to shock them to their cores.

A few days later, Olivia decided to gather up her dilapidated clothes—along with her white ankle socks—and dump them in the trash bin. She dressed in a new gray suit, which she hoped made her look older and even a little wiser, although she doubted a suit could accomplish all that. She didn't want to look too young or vulnerable. She needed to be full of forgiveness but not full of weakness. Mrs. Adder pounced on anything that looked like a frightened mouse.

But, of course, Noah could be right—she could have let the hound of heaven catch up with her. Perhaps redemption had come to the Adder house. Olivia had always prayed it would be true.

When a knock came to the back door, she opened it knowing it would be Noah.

He looked at her. "You look wonderful. Very professional."

"Really? Thank you. I just don't want to look...small today." *Especially not on my fortieth birthday.*

"Trust me, you don't. You look perfect. By the way, last night I did look up Mrs. Adder's address on my computer. She does live at the same address you gave me. Now, let's just hope she'll be at home."

"Someday you'll have to show me how to do that—looking things up online," Olivia said. "I know so little about it all."

"I meant to ask you about Finney's computer and TVs."

"There aren't any. Well, there's a small TV in one of the bedrooms, but Finney didn't want them in the house. He said all that technology would be an intruder in his life, like a thief of his time."

"Hmm. Unusual response, since computers are supposed to be time-savers," Noah said. "So, you've never used a computer?"

"At the public library some, but only a little."

Noah shook his head. "That's probably why coming into this house felt like I was going back in time... way back."

"Is that a bad thing?"

"Not when *you're* here."

"Okay." She smiled all the way to her heart. "You've redeemed yourself."

"So, are you ready?"

"I think so."

"You know, this is quite a leap of faith for you today."

"Yes, it is," Olivia said, picking up her purse off the table. "Let's just pray there's not a cliff waiting for us just beyond that leap."

Noah drove while Olivia tried gallantly not to wring her hands—but failed. *Oh, Lord, I need Your help.* Would Mrs. Adder open the door and then slam it shut in their faces? Would the older woman give them a moment to talk, to try to understand the past?

When the miles were spent and they were on the right Houston street—very near Mrs. Adder's residence— Olivia strained to see the house up ahead. She knew it well. Too well. It was a small, two-story gray house with peeling paint and no shutters on the windows or flower beds in the front to make it seem friendlier. It was walls and windows, but it had never been a home. "It's the one with the couch on the porch and the tattered American flag by the door."

Noah pulled up in the tiny driveway and parked. "Bleak house."

"Right. The outside is nicer than the inside."

"Oh, wow. Really?"

"It was just a place to live. And not even that, really."

Noah touched her shoulder. "I'm sorry you grew up in such an unhappy place."

"Me too." Olivia stared at the house—the bare windows stared back like vacant eyes, glaring at her just like Mrs. Adder always did. "I guess we'd better go in."

Noah rested his hands over Olivia's thrashing fingers and didn't let them go until she'd calmed herself.

"We can wait here as long as you like," Noah said. "In fact, we don't have to go in. We can back away right now if going home is what you want. It's up to you... how much you can handle."

"Thank you for that." Those two words—*going home*. Nothing sounded better to Olivia, but she knew she had to follow through with her plan, or she would always be disappointed in herself. And the opportunity to talk to Mrs. Adder might never come again. "I'm ready." She opened the car door. "Let's do it."

"Stay put. I'll come and get that door for you."

Noah came around to her side and offered Olivia his hand.

"Thanks."

He led her to the front door as he glanced around. Noah was probably looking at the landscaping, or the lack of it. Mrs. Adder always did have more mud than grass.

Moments later, when they were on the front porch, Olivia breathed another prayer, looked at Noah to take in the encouragement of his warm smile and then pushed the doorbell. Wind chimes jingled in the breeze, but they sounded more ghostly than welcoming.

They waited, but no one came to the door. "Maybe she's gone to the store." Olivia looked at her watch. "Although it's not ten yet."

Olivia rang the bell again, and then something

thumped inside the house. She took one small step backward, her breath catching in her throat. "Lord, have mercy," she whispered. Could she really do it? Really look into those shiny darting eyes as black as coal?

A clicking sound echoed behind the door. Probably the dead bolt. The door cracked open and eyes peered out from the darkened living room. It was her—Mrs. Adder. Once a person witnessed Mrs. Adder's forbidding stare, no one could forget it.

Chapter 8

"Don't be ringing that bell like it was a toy." From the darkness of her cave, Mrs. Adder squinted into the light. "What'cha want?" The sound coming from the woman's mouth hadn't changed in twenty years—a person could slice a melon with the sharp, metallic edge of her voice.

"We're not here to sell you anything. I'm Olivia Lamington. Do you remember me?"

"Oh." The woman blinked a few times, her thin lids closing over watery eyes. She looked Olivia up and down and then huffed. "Course I remember you. So, what'd you come back fer?"

"I just thought we could visit for a while."

An odd smell escaped through the opening in the doorway, a combination of malodorous clothes and stale cologne.

"Who's that you brought with you?" Her forefinger, which was as crooked as a broken twig, jutted out at them.

"I'm Noah Bromfeld. Olivia's boyfriend," he said with a decisive tone.

Olivia glanced over at Noah. His chin had a firm tilt, and he seemed pretty serious about his admission. Her face flushed, but she'd never been prouder to stand next to anyone in her life. "May we come in for a little while?"

"Guess so. But only for a bit. I keep real busy with my daytime dramas on TV." The door eased open and, after kicking a floor rug out of the way, Mrs. Adder backed away for them to enter.

Olivia and Noah stepped into the tiny entry and followed Mrs. Adder into the living area. "Can't offer you any coffee or tea. Don't keep the stuff around. But I got some whiskey if you want it. You're old enough, I reckon."

"No, thank you." The house looked the same, only drabber, if that were possible. The green marble clock still sat on the tiny mantel as it had when she was growing up. It was the only thing of value that Mrs. Adder had ever owned, but now, years later, the second hand on the clock lurched forward as if it were in pain with every tick. The doleful strains of a country song whined faintly from the kitchen.

Olivia's gaze landed on the sight she'd wanted to avoid but couldn't—the broom closet under the stairs. It had always been a box of a room and always smelled like things that needed to be swept away, which was most likely the reason the older woman had often banished her there. The closet's missing lightbulb, which Mrs. Adder removed because she claimed it was a waste of electricity, kept Olivia engulfed in semidarkness. In the daylight hours, after her eyes adjusted, there was usually a sliver of light that came from under the door. At night a faint rosy glow had sometimes appeared unexplained.

Mrs. Adder motioned for them to sit on the couch. She sat across from them on a recliner. The older woman was just that—much older—and she hadn't aged well. Her skin looked like thin, crumpled parchment, and her eyes appeared more deep set than ever. "So," she said, slapping her hands on her legs, "tell me again why you came?"

"For a visit. I thought we might get to know each other better…as adults."

"Adults. Humph." Mrs. Adder moved an open can of pork and beans away from her as if Olivia might steal it. A fork rested inside the can, so apparently Mrs. Adder still enjoyed her habit of eating beans out of the can while she watched TV.

"All right." The old woman gave her a slow, assessing nod. "Since you came, I'm gonna give you a little present. The truth." She sniffed the air. "I never wanted you. No. It was my husband, Henry. His dream was to take in a foster child…that is, after Suzette died…our baby girl. Henry and me had started the paperwork, and then he suddenly died of a heart attack. Just like that. So, I was too busy grieving over Henry to stop the foster-care proceedings. And I wanted to honor my husband's wishes, since that's all I had left of him. Just his dream. So, that's how you came to be here living at my house."

Olivia had never once heard that sad story, but, oh, how she wished Mrs. Adder hadn't felt a need to honor her husband's wishes. "I'm sorry for your loss. That's truly tragic, but I'm sure your husband would have understood, you know, had you not wanted to take in a foster child after all."

"I shouldn't have taken you in. That is true. I resented you every day you were here, 'cause you were using the only other bedroom I had...and that bedroom belonged to my sweet Suzette. My baby. You were in *her* place, filling the room with *your* memories. The longer you stayed in her room, the more my baby faded...just like her clothes in the baby chest. Your living in there made it seem like she was dying, slow like...all over again. *You* did that to me. So, I don't appreciate you coming around pretending that you want to visit with me, 'cause I know the real reason you came. To make me feel guilty for something, when it was you who was a daily torment to me."

"Once again, I'm sorry for your grief. I can't even imagine losing a child, a baby. But—"

"No, you can't know the grief. Never."

"But it would help me to know...is that the real reason you made me spend so much time in the broom closet? Because I was in your daughter's bedroom, and you—"

"So what if it was the reason?"

Noah tensed next to her. She knew he was having a hard time remaining silent.

Olivia stared over toward the closet again. It was an ordinary thing to see, really—a wooden door, which opened to a small closet under the staircase. In fact, the sight of it was as innocent looking as a nursery bed, and yet it made her spirit tremble with a thousand conflicting emotions, feelings she still couldn't fully understand. She scooted forward on the couch, desperate for the older woman to understand her. "Thank you for telling me the truth. It helps to know, to understand. But in spite of your great loss, I wish you could have loved me. I wish—"

"I wish this. Oh, I wish that. This ain't no fairy-tale life, girly. You'd just as well wake up to it. That's my words of wisdom for the day. Now if you'll 'scuse me, I've got my favorite soap coming on." She smiled, showing a row of yellowed teeth.

Noah rose. "So, there's no apology for abusing and tormenting an innocent young girl?" He straightened his shoulders and put his hands on his hips.

"Ow, the big man speaks. Well, I'm so sorry, but there'll be no apology coming from these lips." Mrs. Adder reached for the remote control and pointed it at the TV. "You're in my way, bud. I need to watch my soap."

Olivia got up off the couch to leave. "Before I go, I will say this. I wanted us to be a family so badly. I was an abandoned child eager for your attention, your affection, anything that said you cared about me. I was yearning for a home in this world, a safe place where I could rest my head and not fear each day, each hour. But you, Mrs. Adder, made my life a den of misery."

Fires of rage burned in Mrs. Adder's eyes. "I want you out of my house, and you can take your boyfriend with you." A bit of spittle spewed from her mouth as she spoke. "If you don't go, I'll call the police."

"We will go when Olivia says we will go." Noah walked right up to the recliner. "I too am sorry for you and your husband's loss, but to take out your sorrow on a child left in your care is unthinkable. You are beyond help if you think that what you did to Olivia was in any way acceptable behavior for a grown woman. What you are in need of, madam, is some serious prison time. So, I agree. Calling the police is an excellent idea. I would be more than happy to tell the officers how, year after year, you abused an innocent child." Noah picked up the phone on the end table and handed it to Mrs. Adder.

She grabbed the phone out of his hand and slammed it down.

Time to go. Olivia glanced over at the closet one last time. Closure would come more easily if she could just have one more look inside—not as a child but as an adult. Olivia rose and, before she could talk herself out of it, strode to the broom closet under the stairs.

"What are you doing, you little brat?" Mrs. Adder asked.

Olivia didn't answer her as she stared into the small, darkened space. A broom and a mop and a bucket, but still no bulb. No light. It still looked the same. Maybe smaller, but just as lonely looking as ever.

Scenes of the woman's accusations came back to Olivia in a flood of memories. She swallowed and breathed and willed herself not to be ill. Her heart nearly pounded right out of her chest as her spirit spiraled into that old feeling of dejection. In a flash, she was a child again and crouching in the closet in a ball of pain—inside that murky space, feeling the sting of banishment and yet the relief of being away from the woman's bitter tongue. She felt the profound loss of family, but she knew the loving arms of her Creator. God had found her there in that small space, a place where no person wanted to go. But God did. Redemption had come to Olivia in spite of everything, and that rescue—that magnificent deliverance of her soul— was more than enough. For now and for all time.

Olivia turned to the older woman with resolve. "Mrs. Adder." She folded her hands calmly in front of her. "I doubt we will ever see each other again, so I want you to know that I forgive you for all you did to me. And all you didn't do. I forgive you, Mrs. Adder, for everything." Her hands no longer trembled. Olivia smiled, because she knew in her heart she meant every word of it.

"Well, I never asked for your forgiveness. Can't see how it changes anything." Mrs. Adder turned on the TV with her remote and stared at the screen.

Olivia walked toward the front of the house. Noah had his hand on her back and opened the door for her. When they were outside, Noah asked, "You okay?"

"Yes."

He put his arm around her anyway.

"I don't know what I expected. But, in spite of the woman's venom, she had tears in her eyes as I left. I am not mistaken. So, there's always hope. The hound of heaven may get to her yet."

A twinkle of merriment passed between them, which

bloomed into grins of joy. Olivia let out a chuckle, and then they burst out laughing all the way to the car. Soon, they were nestled safely inside the car like two doves in a nest. "Thank you for standing up for me in there."

Noah shook his head and grinned. "I have to admit I really was itching for her to call the police."

"But in a way, I'm glad she didn't. It would have only muddied the water, since I'm decades too late turning her in to the authorities. I'm finally ready to move on. I did what I set out to do—to talk to her as a woman and not a child. And to gain some kind of understanding and closure. I never knew about the child who'd died and the vow she made to her husband."

"It's a tragic story, but there's no excuse for the way she treated you," Noah said. "None at all."

"You're right, of course. And I know I will never be able to fully forget all that she did to me, but forgiveness was in my hands. That was one thing I could give her, even if she didn't want it."

"By the way…" Noah donned a sheepish expression. "I'm sorry I introduced myself as your boyfriend. I realize that was presumptuous and pushy, but I couldn't let that woman get the upper hand."

Olivia grinned. "No problem." But had his bold declaration come only out of a need to support her in front of Mrs. Adder, or was there more at play? And should she be applauding a deeper connection with Noah or discouraging it? What would Finney say if he were alive? But then she wasn't sure that Finney's opinion held much weight anymore.

As they drove away, Olivia shook off her negative

musings and said, "Through the years, I didn't drive into Houston very often, so this is a different kind of day in many ways."

Noah looked over at her and smiled. "Would you like to do something special?"

"Yes, yes. I would. It would be a great way to celebrate my birthday."

The car slowed. Astonishment lit Noah's face. "*This* is your birthday? No kidding?"

"No kidding. My fortieth."

"Really?" Noah pulled onto the freeway and headed toward downtown. "Why didn't you tell me before?"

"I don't know. Well, I guess I do know. I didn't want you to feel obligated to make my day special. And too, I thought after talking to Mrs. Adder I wouldn't feel like celebrating. But you know what? I was wrong. There is some cheering to do. I've officially let go of my past as if I'd written it out, stuffed it in a bottle and thrown it into the sea."

"Beautifully said. So, we need to do something wonderful, then. Anything you'd like. A day of pleasures for Olivia."

"Really, a whole day of treats? For me?" She wrapped her fingers into a little bundle and giggled.

"Absolutely. Anything you'd like, and I'm buying."

"Well, I've never been to a 3-D, IMAX movie or shopping in Uptown. I'd love to eat some really good Vietnamese food, and I'd like to top off the day with one of those foamy mocha things at Starbucks that I saw advertised one time. I always dreamed of going there."

"You're kidding. You've never been to Starbucks?"

"Never once." She rolled down the window and hollered, "I'm going to Starbucks!"

He shook his head. "You need to get out more, Olivia. And I'm going to make sure you do."

They both grinned, and they were the kinds of smiles that glowed with the knowledge that something unique was happening between them, something not to be missed. But the sunniest part of the day was when Noah had introduced himself as her boyfriend. That could not be forgotten if she tried. In fact, she'd be able to live off that surprise for a long time to come.

When the day was over and the hours had been filled with Noah, she finally rested her head on her pillow. What a day. What had started out wretched had ended with great joy—and promise. A birthday she would never forget.

But in life, unfortunately, glad tidings were sometimes followed by bad news. Perhaps what she'd gained with Noah in the past several days would be lost. She hoped not. In the very short time they'd been together, he'd managed to find a place in her heart, and she wasn't sure if that place—should he choose to go away—could ever be filled by anyone else. Yes, she wanted to be more to Noah than just a lost piece in his elaborate jigsaw puzzle—so much more.

Olivia fluffed her pillow and snuggled down into the king-size bed. She'd moved all her belongings into the largest bedroom on the second floor—the one that had its own balcony—to celebrate her birthday and her entry into a new life without the confines of the closet and without the rebukes of Mrs. Adder in her head.

She really had healed enough from her past to appreciate a large and lovely room that was filled with pastels
and lacy decor—a room as pretty as an Easter bonnet.

But with the spaciousness of the bedroom came an
ache—a loneliness. Not just in the bedroom but the
whole house. There was far too much quiet. A house
as huge as Bromfeld Manor was meant to be filled with
laughter and love.

And children.

Except for a fleeting thought or two, she'd never
imagined having children with any particular man before. But she did now, even though she was probably
too old for such a blessing. Perhaps if no children came,
though, they could adopt a few kids. What a joy that
would be and, unlike Mrs. Adder, she would count each
of them as a treasure from God. She let those thoughts
twirl happily in her head like a merry-go-round until
she nodded off into a deep slumber.

Then sometime after nightfall, Olivia awakened in
her bed with a gasp. What was that sound? Had someone whispered to her in the darkness, or was it a dream?
She tried to sit up in bed, but the sheets had a strangle-
hold on her. She turned on the light, unwound the bedding from her legs and wiped the perspiration from
her forehead.

Everything looked less scary in the soft glow of her
lamp, but she couldn't shake the uneasiness. Maybe
it was just her first night in a strange new bedroom.
That had to be it, and yet something else stirred in her
spirit—a niggling sensation that her world was about
to change. Again.

* * *

The next morning the sun rose looking like a big egg yolk in the sky, and the pork sausages sputtered and rolled in the cast-iron skillet. None of the strange night terrors came visiting Olivia again. It was going to be another wonderful day with Noah. They'd planned to spend the day working on the cottage together. But just as breakfast was almost ready, a knock came on the back door. Assuming it was Noah, Olivia opened it readily without even looking.

Lucile Barnes, the former housekeeper, stood on the back porch step, looking as merrily rotund as ever and wearing her usual attire—a dress in the form of a tent. "Hi, Livy."

"Mrs. Barnes, how nice to see you. What brings you back to the manor?"

"Oh, I forgot my favorite hat. And please, I really do wish you'd call me Lucile." She scratched her head. "I've been missing my hat and realized I'd left it here. I think I stuffed it in that bottom drawer inside the pantry."

"I'll get it for you." Olivia opened the door wider. "Please come in."

The older woman peered inside. "Well, I'll just come in for a bit." She wiped off her shoes on the mat and brought a wake of smells with her, but mostly the odor of mothballs.

Olivia found the woman's hat easily and handed it to her, but the straw sunbonnet appeared to be on the last day of its life.

"That breakfast smells good." Lucile licked her lips.

"Are you hungry?"

"Well, I'd never want to be an imposition, but I—"

"Please. You're welcome to have some breakfast with me."

"Maybe another time."

"Why didn't you knock on the front door?" Olivia asked.

"Oh, you know me. I'm just a back-door kind of woman. I didn't think it was my place to sashay up to the front door like a real guest."

"But you *are* a real guest." Until now, Olivia hadn't realized how much she'd missed the older woman's company.

Lucile leaned over the skillet and breathed in. "For somebody who's had no formal training in the culinary arts, well, your sausages and eggs smell almost divine. But it's too bad you don't have any of those little fingerling potatoes to go with it." She shifted her false teeth around inside her mouth, which was always an unsettling sight. "Tell you what—I don't mind taking some of that breakfast off your hands if you could make me up a little to-go plate."

"Sure. I have plenty to share." Olivia scooped up the scrambled eggs and a few of the sausages and put them in a covered dish. Fortunately, she'd bought enough food to make another batch.

Lucile zipped her hand along the counter and looked at her finger. "So, how you doing in this big old house? I'd be petrified right out of my boomers if I so much as heard the scratching of a branch on my windowpane at night."

"I'm okay."

"I see you got your memory ribbon on. What are you trying not to forget?"

It was something connected to Noah, but Olivia wasn't sure how much to tell Lucile about him, since she'd always been as tender toward gossip as she was toward sausages and eggs. "Finney's son came back. He's living in the cottage, but I intend to give him Bromfeld Manor, since he's the rightful owner."

Lucile reared back, scowling. "Noah Bromfeld? Fiddledeedee. He's dead. Died of some hideous disease in a foreign land."

"I thought so too, but it wasn't true." Olivia set the covered dish in a paper bag.

"Ow." Lucile's eyes widened. "That's quite a kettle of fish."

"What do you mean?"

"Well, I remember hearing old Finney saying, just like it was yesterday, mind you, that when his son was growing up he called him a little sneak of a boy. Finney said there wasn't anything the boy couldn't pull off or entice someone into with that silver tongue of his. He always said that Noah was destined to be a master shyster when he grew up. So, hope that Noah isn't finagling his way into your life to get what Finney gave you fair and square."

"No, of course not. I don't see it that way at—"

"Eh-heh-heh." Lucile waggled her chubby finger in Olivia's face. "I'm just warning you. I can't do the heeding for you. You know what happened to the queen of hearts in the nursery rhyme, don't you?"

"No, I never learned any of them in school."

Lucile donned a somber expression. "Maybe that's best." Then she perked up, stuffed her hat on top of her untamed gray curls and elbowed Olivia affectionately. "Hey, I kind of missed you, little Livy. I might drop in from time to time, and I might even come to the front door."

"Sure, you're welcome anytime."

Then Lucile took her sausages and eggs—without the beloved fingerlings—and hobbled out the back door, mumbling to herself and shaking her finger in the air to no one in particular.

Hmm. Finney had always called Lucile an odd bird, and even though Olivia didn't like to think unkind things about people, she had to admit there was some truth to his assessment. But if she chose to believe Finney about Lucile, should she believe him about his son? Surely the bitterness Finney felt toward his wife had simply spilled over onto his son. For now, Olivia dismissed the accusation against Noah and pulled out another carton of eggs.

Chapter 9

The pleasant weeks of spring with their cooling breezes had flowed into summer like leaves floating down a lazy river. The weather had continued to stay fairly mild and dry, which Noah counted as a huge blessing in Southeast Texas, where it could be blazing hot and mercilessly humid. But none of the fine weather could compare to what he liked to call his "sweet days of Olivia."

Noah sat down on the wooden bench and stared at the caretaker's cottage. The two of them had accomplished a great deal in the past several months, giving the little house what seemed like a hundred small repairs and upgrades. The cottage was now more livable, and, fortunately, the stocks in Finney's journal had indeed been valuable, so it allowed them the luxury of working on the estate for a while before settling into more permanent work. But, best of all, he'd gotten to spend the time with Olivia—his Olivia.

He smiled, thinking of the curtains she'd sewn and how she'd put them up with such care. It was the same way she tended to everything around her. Like the injured bird she'd found at the edge of the woods. Olivia had fed it, coaxed it and loved it until it could fly on its own. In spite of the terrible things that had been done to her as a child, she was still full of affection for life—and for him.

Noah rested his arms across the back of the bench. Olivia had come to mean more to him than he'd ever imagined. She was a font of delight. He chuckled. What a thing to think—font of delight. He was turning into mush. Olivia Lamington had transformed an old cynic into a lover of love again.

In fact, in some ways that he couldn't fully understand, he thought he'd been connected to her even before they'd met. Could that be true? Was it destiny? He had no idea. But he knew one thing.

It was love.

There could be no denying it now—his heart had submitted to it willingly. A lifetime with Olivia would never be enough to hear her laughter, to be tangled in her embrace and to be lost in her smile. Their years together would seem all too brief, even if they'd found each other as teenagers. Oh, if only that could have been true. If only they'd met twenty years ago. He'd wasted too much time with women who seemed more interested in their own mirrored reflections than in creating a real life.

One woman in particular came to mind—Hedda Mouser—a woman who could not be compared to Olivia. The contrast was too great. But perhaps he should have been more forthcoming about his strange history with Hedda. Then again, the young woman had not come around to stir up any trouble, so it was best not to bother Olivia with too much of the past.

Noah pulled out his harmonica and fingered it. Since he occasionally succumbed to gloomy feelings, it was good that he'd finally stopped reading his father's journals. They were too full of bitterness, and Noah was finally ready to let go of those early years. He was prepared to forgive his father for his lack of affection and his mother for her unfaithfulness. No doubt Olivia was what inspired him to move forward, since it was easier to gaze into the future when lit with the glow from Olivia's face. In fact, maybe it was time for another romantic evening in Houston.

"Noah," Olivia hollered from somewhere behind him on the path. "I made two apple pies. And this time I remembered to add the sugar."

He chuckled.

Olivia came running up to him, looking quite fetching in one of the dresses he'd bought for her online. All her outfits, he discovered, had to have pockets for hiding her hands and for storing the now-infamous red memory ribbon she kept in her pocket—that was, when it wasn't around her wrist to remind her of something important.

Instead of sitting down, Olivia stood next to him and touched his hair, much the way she'd done that

first day in the kitchen, when he was somewhere between the dreaming and the waking world. At the time
he had been too blinded by grief and anger to see who
Olivia was. He'd been too foolish to see that she would
become his jewel, his wonder and his joy.

Noah scooted over and patted the seat next to him.

Olivia sat down on the bench, and when Noah pointed
toward a clearing behind them, she followed his gaze.

"Do you see that meadow over there where the sun
makes the grass look like gold?"

"Yes, it's a pretty spot, although I didn't used to
think so. I used to like the woods more than the open
meadow." Olivia rested her chin on his shoulder. "But
I see beauty and wonder in unexpected places now."

He smiled, hoping she'd tucked a double meaning
into her reply. "I'm going to build you a rose garden
there."

"Really?"

"Yes, really. And I'll make a pond in the middle with
an arched wooden bridge. It'll be a kissing bridge...*our*
kissing bridge."

"Especially when the stars are out at night," Olivia
said. "And practically speaking, you could use it like a
sample to show off all the wonderfully creative things
you can do once you've started your landscaping company."

"I hadn't even thought of that angle. You'll make a
good partner in the business. By the way, now that the
repairs on the cottage are almost finished, I made some
inquiries around Gardenia about starting the landscape
company."

"And?"

"This area really is growing, like you said, and there only seems to be one other local company that provides landscaping services to this area. So, we should think about it more seriously now, don't you think?"

"We should, yes. Bromfeld Landscape Design has a nice ring to it."

Ring, indeed. He grinned. "Yes, it does. By the way, how do you do it?"

"Do what?"

"How do you romance the sun that way?" Noah asked. "Your face is just as golden as that meadow over there."

"Stop. You're making me blush."

"I like to make you blush. It's delightful."

Olivia shook her head at him. "How you do go on."

"No, I'm not kidding. You, Olivia Lamington, are the love song so beautiful it makes one's heart yearn for more." He slapped his hand over his heart. "You're a sunset that's rendered so exquisitely on a canvas that it makes a person think they've had a glimpse of paradise. You are the fine—"

"Noah Bromfeld, have you been drinking something stronger than my sweet tea?"

"No." Noah laughed. "Why won't you believe me?"

"Because it's hyperbole."

"No." He reached over to her cheek and turned her to look at him. "It's called a compliment."

"All right." She picked at the fabric on her dress. "Thank you." Then she raised an eyebrow at him. "But there's something else going on here. I can tell. You look like you've had your hands in the cookie jar before dinner."

"I was just wondering if you'd like to take a trip into Houston tomorrow. We've been working so hard fixing up the estate I thought it might be fun for a change."

"It would be nice. I decided I love Vietnamese food, so could we eat that again?"

"Are you sure you wouldn't like to try something different?"

"What did you have in mind?" Olivia grinned.

"There's a great South American place in the Uptown area. They have an upstairs floor that's made to look like you're dining in an elegant tree house."

"Ow...sounds romantic."

"That's exactly what I'm hoping for." The moment was perfect. Perhaps too perfect. He thought of the snake in the woodpile, but that was just his melancholy temperament running loose again. He brushed off any more gloomy inclinations and chose to embrace the moment. He picked a wildflower near the bench and slipped it into her hair. "And will you press this flower into one of your favorite novels?"

"I might."

"Which one will it be?" Noah asked.

Olivia grinned. *"Great Expectations."*

Nice. Since the timing was more than ripe for a kiss, Noah had leaned over to do that very thing when the high-pitched bellow of the widow Barnes pierced the air like a bird of prey homing in on its morning feast.

Olivia turned around. "Hey there, Lucile."

"Greetings, all," the woman said. "Lucile Barnes has arrived."

Noah squeezed the bridge of his nose, since he detected a headache coming on. Then he prayed to clean up his thoughts. Every time he saw the woman—which as of late had become more frequent—his mind kept screaming the word *battle-ax*. *God, forgive me, but that woman is painting my Christianity right into a corner.* Over the past few days, Lucile had been conveniently dropping by just before mealtime or on Olivia's baking day. What did she need now? A few more pies? Perhaps the only way he'd be guaranteed some time alone with Olivia was to drive her into Houston—far away from the meddlesome antics of the widow Barnes.

Olivia gave Lucile a warm hug.

Noah could have sworn he heard the older woman mumble something about "Ring Around the Rosie" as she pointed to him. He dismissed the possible slur and gave the older woman a two-finger salute from his bench. "Hello, Mrs. Barnes."

Lucile tipped her straw hat at him. "Hello, sonny boy." Then she gave Olivia's cheek an affectionate pinch. "Hope I'm not wearing out my welcome coming here."

"Don't be silly," Olivia said. "Of course not."

"Oh, that Livy is a precious one," Lucile said to Noah. "You'd better keep her closer than a handkerchief next to your heart. Eh?"

"That's certainly my intention." *If given half a chance.*

Lucile turned to Olivia. "I was just wondering. I need to go to my doctor in Houston to get some new false teeth. Mine are getting old and yeller." She chortled at her joke. "And I need someone to drive me there and back. You know how scared I am of that freeway driving. It's like a bunch of lunatics let loose from the asylum." She adjusted her clothes, giving her elastic waistband a good snap.

"Of course I can take you," Olivia said. "When's your appointment?"

"Tomorrow afternoon."

Noah raked his fingers down his face and groaned. Loudly.

Both of the women stared at him, looking wounded. There it was again—he'd been shamed into dust.

Noah rose from the bench. His plans to spend some serious time with Olivia had been railroaded, but with his one lapse in manners he'd become Mr. Surly to his beloved. "I'm sorry. It's just that, well, I'd planned to take Olivia into Houston tomorrow."

"Well, then, how lucky for me," Lucile said. "I guess it would be okay for you to tag along with us, Noah, but it's probably going to be boring for you. You know, two women just talking about false teeth all day."

He cleared his throat. "But that's not what—"

"Of course Noah wants to help." Olivia flashed him another questioning expression. "What we had planned can wait for another day."

"Good." Lucile smiled, bulldozing right over Noah's anguish entirely. "Then it's settled."

"You're right," Noah said. "Just the two of you might be best. I'll stay home and work on redoing the shrubbery beds in the back of the cottage."

"Good thinking." Lucile shook her finger in the air.

His plans had taken a nosedive again. This was definitely not turning out to be a paint-your-house-purple kind of day. Sadly, for now, he stopped fingering the ring in his pocket. Yes, when it came to his relationship with Olivia, sometimes he felt that forces were working against him—and those forces usually showed up in the person of Lucile Barnes.

"I don't know what I'd do without you now, Livy," Mrs. Barnes went on to say. "You know the way you help me with this and that. Without you I'd be a hapless old woman sitting in my bathrobe and watching reruns of some awful sitcom."

Olivia chuckled and gave the older woman another hug.

Then Lucile pointed a plump finger toward the cottage. "Noah, I think you said you're redoing the beds in the back of the cottage, but I spy a dead shrub along the front. It'd be best if you'd get rid of that, too."

"Yes, it's crossed my mind," Noah said.

"Good." Lucile grinned, which always drew attention to the line of hair on her upper lip. "So, looks like you'll have plenty to do, sonny boy, while we're gone to the city."

He sighed. "Yes, thanks, Mrs. Barnes."

"Fiddledeedee. You never need to thank me. Whoop, said a rhyme, made a dime, as my mother used to say." She giggled. "You know, my gal friends always tell me, although I'm not one to crow about myself…but they say that I have a real gardening eye. So sharp and resolute, they say I possess the steely sagacity of a Texas turkey vulture. Yes, indeed."

"Well, can't argue with that," Noah said.

Olivia drove around to the garage and pulled inside. It was only four o'clock, and yet it felt as if it had been several days in one. Lucile's personality could be appreciated in small increments, but a whole day of gossip and cackling and the minuscule details of her dental appointment as well as her new dream of having a bunionectomy had completely worn her out.

And on top of everything, she missed Noah. She'd felt terrible about blowing off their special day. He'd planned a wonderful evening, and she'd dismissed him with an ugly glare right in front of Lucile. That had been so unkind. Surely she could have handled the moment with more diplomacy. But since this was her first romantic relationship, she was in deep water, so much so that her feet could barely touch the bottom. How would she ever swim back to shore if the need should arise? But Noah appeared faithful—unlike his mother, who seemed to have dismissed fidelity as easily as a twist of her wrist.

She opened the car door and went into the kitchen for some tea. Or maybe something stronger. Maybe she'd splurge and have some espresso with that newfangled machine Noah had bought her. The caffeine would keep her awake all night, but it would be worth it. And she'd make enough for Noah and take it to him as a way to say she was sorry.

Olivia opened the cupboard for two espresso cups

and saucers while she pondered Noah's surprise evening. Had he intended to propose? Was that it? Surely
not. Wasn't it too soon? Or was it? She'd grown to love
Noah dearly over their months together, and she wasn't
about to spoil his delight in surprising her. She too
wanted to experience an enchanted evening—a moment
they both would remember for a lifetime, the one she
would tell their children about. That was, if it weren't
too late for them to have a child or two.

Olivia brushed her hand over her lips, remembering
his kisses. The prospect of marrying Noah and sharing
a lifetime with him seemed too good to be true, and yet
maybe it would be within her reach. She thought of his
face, his features. Noah was such a fine-looking man,
but it was funny that she hadn't noticed how handsome
he was until she loved him.

Olivia loves Noah. She chuckled. Oh, so true, and
wouldn't those words look marvelous carved into the
big oak tree out back? Love had arrived in spite of his
family's past. Although Noah hadn't said the actual
"I love you" words yet, she felt fairly certain that they
would arrive soon. It was a dream she'd been too scared
to hope for, and yet God had seen fit to give her this
joy. With Noah's love, God had redeemed the years the
locus had taken, the years of Mrs. Adder and her harsh
rules and heartless miseries. When had it happened—
this love for Noah? It felt as if she'd always loved him
but she just hadn't known his name yet.

As she moved the cups and saucers to the table, the
doorbell rang. The sound startled her, making her knock
one of the cups off the edge of the counter. It tumbled

onto the ceramic floor and shattered into pieces. She'd have to clean it up later.

Who could that be at the door? It wasn't Noah, since he always came in through the back of the kitchen. When she opened the front door, a woman stood on the porch—a young woman, perhaps in her late twenties, with hair the color of rubies and eyes like emeralds. She had a roundish look around her middle, but, more noticeable than anything, the woman had a heated expression on her face that was rising like mercury in a glass thermometer.

"I'm Hedda Mouser, and you're Olivia Lamington."

"Yes." The woman was a stranger to Olivia, and yet she looked vaguely familiar—eerily so. Had she seen the woman before? Perhaps at the cemetery? An unsettling feeling trickled through her like ink on a pristine tablecloth. "How may I help you?"

"Well, since you're Ms. Lamington, you'll be interested to know that I'm Noah's girlfriend." Ms. Mouser touched her abdomen. "And I'm pregnant with his child."

Chapter 10

Olivia steadied herself on the door frame. Her head went so dizzy she thought she might black out. *Oh, dear Lord, have mercy. This cannot be happening.*

The woman took a step closer to the door. "I've been waiting for this moment."

Olivia suddenly realized the woman hadn't been overweight but was wearing a maternity outfit. When she ran her hand along her form, Olivia could see the small mound below her abdomen—that she was with child. "I'm sorry for your…your…confusion," she stammered. "Perhaps you mean some other Noah. He would never—"

"There's no mistake," she said plainly.

Olivia's stomach churned. How could joy turn into sorrow so quickly? The woman's confession was too horrible to consider. Had Noah misrepresented himself as a man who had no romantic ties? She said, "But this is not—"

"Olivia," Noah called to her from somewhere in the house. He'd come looking for her. Should she invite the woman in? Confront Noah? What else could she do?

"Would you like to come inside for a moment? If any of this is true, we'll know soon enough."

Noah arrived around the corner as Hedda strolled into the entry hall. He halted the moment he saw her. "Hedda?" From his expression, he obviously knew the woman, but he wasn't overjoyed to see her.

"Hello, Noah."

Noah shook her hand but then quickly pulled away from her. "What brings you here?" His tone was neither welcoming nor unkind.

"I came to visit you and Ms. Lamington." Hedda turned to Olivia. "She's invited me in, which is good, since we three have something to discuss."

Noah's hands went to his hips. "I can't imagine what—"

"I think you need to hear her out," Olivia said to Noah. Not knowing what to do with her hands, she clasped them behind her back. "Why don't we all go into the sunroom?" She tried to keep the quiver out of her voice, but it wasn't going to be easy. "Please go ahead, Ms. Mouser. It's through those French doors to your left."

Hedda strolled through the entry hall, looking around with obvious awe at the stately first impression that Bromfeld Manor offered its visitors.

While Hedda was busy gawking, Noah took hold of Olivia by the elbow and whispered, "What's wrong?"

"You will know soon enough." She eased her elbow from his grasp, even though it pained her to do so.

When they were all three seated, Hedda said, "You mentioned this house, Noah, but you never told me how majestic it is with the high ceilings and archways and gilding. Oh, and I *so* can see a bride gliding down that grand staircase." She chattered on to herself like a child on Christmas morning. "It seems like the kind of house that is full of secrets, too. I'll bet it even has a door that opens right out of the wall with a hidden passageway and everything."

"Sorry. No hidden passageways." Noah crossed his arms. "So, what brings you here?"

Hedda's wrist twisted against her shoulder until she looked as though she was causing herself pain. "I came to tell you…"

"Yes?"

"Well, I came to tell you that I'm pregnant…with your child. We can have the family you always wanted—"

"What?" Noah shot up out of his chair, knocking it over. "That's a lie, and you know it." He looked back and forth at both women, and when they remained serious, he added, "What you're saying is impossible. You know very well we didn't…that we were never intimate in *that* way."

"We were intimate all right." Hedda gathered her hands below her abdomen, which flaunted the fact that she was expecting a child.

Noah stood silent, his fingers pinching the bridge of his nose.

Olivia swallowed the awful taste in her mouth. All the gossip that Lucile had told her about Noah rushed back in a flood of accusations. At the time, the warnings from the older woman had seemed mischievous and spiteful, but could Lucile's dark tidings be true? Did it all make perfect sense, and she'd been too naive to catch on? That was assuming she chose to believe this Hedda woman. She didn't know what to think. It was her word against his. Only three beings knew the truth—Noah and Hedda—and God. She'd been left out.

Noah gazed at her with one of the most heart-wrenching expressions she'd ever seen. She was breaking his heart, but she didn't know what to do. Was it all an act as Lucile had said? The older woman couldn't remember her own Social Security number, but she could recall with detail many of the derogatory remarks Finney had made against his son. Regrettably, Olivia had listened to the stories, mostly of how smooth-talking Noah had been growing up. What had he said about her—that she was a sunset rendered so exquisitely on a canvas that it made a person think they'd had a glimpse of paradise? Were his words just more of his youthful folly?

Slowly, Noah righted his chair and sat down. "Please tell me you don't believe Hedda. I must hear it from you now." He leaned toward Olivia.

"I'm not sure what to believe," Olivia whispered with aching honesty. Her chin quivered, but she didn't know if her emotion came from the pain over a possible betrayal or the fear that Noah would leave with Hedda.

Noah took in a deep breath and turned to Hedda. "I know you have a thing for drama. So, if this is a performance, you're believable, but the show is over."

"How can you be so heartless?" Hedda's face flamed red. "I thought deep down you still loved me. I'm carrying your child, Noah. I know you'll want to do what's right in God's eyes and marry me."

Noah lowered his head to his hands, then he suddenly looked at Hedda and said, "I won't leave Olivia, no matter what you say." He rose again and paced around her chair, raking his fingers through his hair. "I know your game. You wanted to find a way to live in Bromfeld Manor. Just so you know, this big old place has more junk than antiques. The tapestries are moth-eaten, and it's fallen into a pathetic state of semiruin. It's going to become a raging money pit, so you can put those grandiose notions to rest. Besides, I don't even legally own the estate. It belongs to Olivia. Right now I live in the caretaker's cottage."

Hedda seemed shocked by the news, but when she recovered, she said, "No. I want you, Noah. Only you. That's all I've ever wanted." She glanced around the room. "But I'd be lying if I said this house wouldn't make a good place to raise our son. I can already see a bassinet in this pretty sunroom, and I can almost hear his laughter echoing through these halls. The grounds here are so spacious and peaceful compared to the city. It would be such a nice place to raise a big family. I still have plenty of years to have children, you know." Hedda turned to Olivia with a knowing gaze.

Olivia looked away. The woman was right about one

thing—with Hedda as his wife, there was still time for Noah to have a family. Maybe she should bow out now. Allow the child to be raised in the country with plenty of fresh air and places to run and play. It made sense, though the pain of leaving would be unbearable. Even with Noah's transgression—if it were true—whatever made her think she was worthy of love, anyway? She could almost hear Mrs. Adder's sneering mantra all those years. *You is worth a whole lot of nothing. So plain and ignorant.* She certainly couldn't compete with the lovely Hedda.

Olivia found her voice. "Noah, if you're trying to save me from any heartache, it's not working. I think if what Ms. Mouser says is true, you should admit it and do the right thing. Please don't drive her to desperate measures. And she'd be right. This would be a good place to raise a family." Olivia forced back the tears and said what needed to be said. "I could go. I feel I must. It won't take me long to pack." She rose to go.

Noah rushed to Olivia's side and took hold of her arms. He wanted to hold her close until he'd driven away any thoughts of his disloyalty. He searched her eyes, but they no longer reflected the warmth and joy he'd come to adore in her. "Stay…so I can take the fear from your eyes," he whispered to Olivia.

"Please let me go" was all she said.

Deep inside, his spirit collapsed in grief. What could he do? He could tell her of his love, but considering his family's history in the matter, it was the worst possible moment to pour out his affections. Reluctantly, his fingers released their hold on her, and his arms fell to his sides.

"Noah, listen to Ms. Lamington if you won't listen to me," Hedda said. "She can sense you're lying and that you need to do the right thing."

In spite of Noah's anger, he felt pity for Hedda. The last thing he wanted to do was explain the past in all its details, since Hedda's history was riddled with emotional issues. He didn't want to humiliate her by laying out all her past ailments, by revealing her mental illnesses in front of Olivia, but neither would he allow the woman to destroy his relationship. He was left with no choice but to expose the real Ms. Mouser and beg her to seek psychiatric help. Noah went over to Hedda's chair. "We'll need to talk about *all* of it…now."

"What do you mean?" Hedda cuddled his hand in her own. "I found out it was a boy. Our baby. I've already named him Noah Bromfeld II." She acted as if Noah's sudden closeness was a sign that his resolve had melted. "Put your hand here, so you'll know I'm not lying."

Hedda grasped Noah's hand, and, before he could think of the ramifications of such an unguarded action, he allowed her to place his hand on her bare abdomen.

Noah jerked his hand back.

"See?" Hedda smiled. "I am carrying a baby…your baby."

Hedda was indeed pregnant. That was certain now.

Olivia had edged toward the door, but she stopped and said, "Noah, let me ask you this. You told me about the four different women you'd seriously dated over the years. Linda, Jenny, Suzanna and Elisha, but you'd never mentioned Ms. Mouser. Why not? If what you said is true, and this is not your child, then there should be no real reason to be secretive about your relationship with her. Unless you had something to hide." Her voice shivered on the last words.

Noah wiped the sweat from his brows. Even though he hated to tell the whole story, Hedda had forced his hand. "Stay, Olivia. Hear the rest of the story. As I mentioned before, there is more to say. And, apparently, I need to say it all."

"I didn't tell you about Hedda because I didn't want you to worry that she could be a danger to you in the future." Noah blurted this out so fast he wasn't even sure if he'd said it right.

"How could I be a danger?" Hedda pulled a wad of tissues from her purse and wiped her nose.

Noah scowled at Hedda. "Because you know when we met ten years ago, you were on medication for what the doctors called delusional episodes and psychotic tendencies. Against the doctor's orders you went off your medicine, and then you began believing things about us that weren't true. You meticulously built a whole world of lies around us. We were dating casually, and yet you told people we were engaged to be married. And now, as friends, you've started to build the lies all over again."

"I don't know what you mean." Hedda scrubbed her knuckles against her head.

"You promised me you would go back on your medication. What happened?"

Hedda turned her thumb back and forth on the wicker arm as if grinding it into the chair. "I was on the medicine for a long time, but now I'm pregnant, and I don't want to take anything that could harm our child." Tears streamed down her face.

"Yes, I understand that," Noah said, now pacing the floor, "and I agree if the doctor does. But you need to stop this delusional thinking about the baby."

Hedda's crying turned into heaving sobs until her whole body shook.

"Noah?" Olivia said softly. "We don't want her to get too distressed. We need to think of the baby."

"Yes. You're right." He'd gotten too worked up. In his demand for the truth, Hedda might become overly distressed and injure the child. "So, let's all calm down, okay? I will, too."

"All right." Hedda looked up at him and smiled now, looking like a child herself. "You've changed your hair, Noah. I like it longer like that, even though it must get in your way when you're working on the cottage."

Noah thought about her words. "How do you know I'm working on the cottage? I never told you I've been fixing up that little house." So as not to upset Hedda again, he kept his voice low and tried to sound more curious than accusing. "In fact, you wouldn't know I'd been working on it…unless you've been following me."

Hedda's gaze darted around the room. A look of dread filled her eyes. "Yes, I was following you, because I wanted to find the perfect time to tell you about the baby."

So, it had been Hedda all along—the reason he'd had that uneasy feeling of being watched. He pressed his palm over his forehead. Oh, how he wished he could take away all the mistakes he'd made in his dating life and the way he'd trusted too many of the wrong women. He'd been sorely lacking in discernment and the courage to say no.

Noah looked over at Olivia, imploringly, but she gave no indication whether she was for him or against him. Or if she would ever speak to him again. "I think it's time for you to go home and rest," he told Hedda. "It'll be good for the baby."

"I will go…for now." As she struggled to get up from the chair, Noah took her by the arm and helped her up. "I will think about all you said, and I'll come back tomorrow morning at nine. Well, goodbye for now, Noah." Hedda kissed him on the cheek and walked out of the room without saying any more and without acknowledging Olivia.

"I'll let her out." Noah grazed a finger along Olivia's arm as he left the room. "Promise me you won't go. We have more to discuss. Much more."

Olivia made no reply.

Noah went to the front door to let Hedda out while Olivia stood in the doorway of the sunroom, numb and confused. She wanted to flee or scream or maybe hide in the safety of her attic room. All that she had hoped for had disappeared like some beautiful and exotic bird that was flying away with no means to capture it again.

Olivia gazed out the sunroom windows. The last of the light streamed in, looking warm and welcoming, but her spirit couldn't absorb any of the goodness. She felt as cold and as lonely as an unmarked grave. It was a feeling she knew well from her youth—all too well.

Ah, the sunroom—it had become Olivia's favorite spot in the house, because it was where she'd first met Noah. Their lives had begun here, but now it appeared that it all might end in the same place.

When Noah returned, Olivia didn't look at him directly but, instead, stared at his reflection in one of the windows. His fine sturdy frame had withered some, and he'd taken on the stature of a much older man. Oh, how it grieved her to see the change.

Noah took hold of Olivia and turned her to face him. "Hedda really is going to have a child. I can beg her to have a DNA test when her baby is born, but my innocence won't be proved for many more months." He shook his head. "I know you want to leave me, but please just hear me out. My side of the story. Please?"

Olivia nodded. "All right."

"Good. Do you want to sit down?"

"I'd rather stand."

"Okay." Noah walked over to the closest chair and sat down. "When I first met Hedda ten years ago, I couldn't tell that anything was wrong with her, but as we dated I noticed things, attitudes and comments she'd make that weren't quite right. And on occasion, I'd see a peculiar look in her eyes that told me she wasn't well in her mind. After a few weeks she became scheming and jealous. As I mentioned, at one point she told people we were engaged, even though I'd never proposed."

"What did you say to Hedda?"

"I said a lot, and she seemed to understand, but just

as soon as I was out of the room, she would go right back to her delusions. I wanted to make a clean break, but I didn't want her to spiral into a depression that might become suicidal. So, I told her that I would still be a friend to her if she needed me." Noah paused and frowned as if the scenes were playing in his mind.

"That was kind of you," Olivia said. "What happened?"

"Well, my offer of friendship didn't change anything. Hedda was still so delusional and jealous that the times we were together weren't…normal. So that she could recover, I broke off what was left of our friendship. Then I ran into Hedda right before I came here to Bromfeld Manor. She told me she was back on her medicine. She seemed well-adjusted and busy working at an upscale flower shop. So, when she asked me to go along with her to a movie with some friends, I agreed…but only as a friend. That turned out to be another mistake. I was such a fool. I soon discovered her carefree attitude had only been an act." Noah pushed his hair away from his face. "You know, I can't tell by looking into your eyes if you believe this. Any of it. Do you?"

"I'm trying." And she was doing that very thing with all her heart, but just as she'd misjudged Finney all those years, she couldn't be certain how her relationship with Noah would end. It was like looking into a murky pool—no clear view or answers. Olivia loved him, though—that was certain. Too late to take the feeling back. Even if she had to leave, she would always love Noah. That was one certainty in the midst of all the doubt.

He closed his eyes for a moment as if in prayer and then said, "Thank you for that. For not throwing me out of your house."

"*Your* house." Olivia hugged her middle. "But Hedda *is* pregnant. And I admit she's intense in her rhetoric, but sometimes a woman who is desperate can come off as unbalanced. I understand desperation. I can't help but wonder what I would sound like if I faced those kinds of circumstances...unrequited love."

"But it's more than that. If the baby belongs to another man, can't you see that she would be mentally disturbed?"

"Yes, of course," Olivia said. If *all you say is the truth.*

"Please sit down."

"I can't. I'm sorry." Olivia instead walked across the room and stood by the windows.

Noah came over to her gingerly as if he might frighten her off—the very same way he'd approached the house when they'd first laid eyes on each other months before. "Surely you can tell how I feel about you...that I love you dearly."

"You shouldn't say it. Not now." Olivia had longed for Noah's love—for those very words to spill from his heart—and to tell him of her feelings. But the time wasn't right.

Noah slipped his hands into the pockets of his jeans and gazed down at the floor as if thinking long and hard about her words. "If you don't think you can return my feelings, I won't stay on here. I doubt I would ever heal, but I wouldn't haunt you and hassle you and destroy your chances for future happiness the way Hedda has tried to destroy mine. I wouldn't threaten you or manipulate you. I would simply go, and you would never see me again."

Olivia shuddered. "I see." Fear swelled through her like a boiling storm cloud—since she knew that he could do that very thing—vanish at any time. He'd certainly done it before, for twenty long years. Along with the anxiety, her mind kept coming back to the word *love,* since it was the first time Noah had come so close to saying those words about their relationship. He'd alluded to his affections, but he'd never been prepared to say the word until today. It was a sentiment full of tenderness and giddy delights, and yet now it felt like a burden instead of a joy.

Noah reached up and fingered the latch—the one that had always been broken. "I guess you think under these circumstances that I'm trying to sway you my way by telling you of my feelings, of my love. That it was just a cheap trick to make you believe me."

Olivia's spirit wilted hearing Noah's words. She moved another step closer to him, wanting to feel his warmth—that connection she'd grown to love. "Please don't feel that way."

But just as she was about to reach out to him, he went on to say, "The thing is, I feel sorry for the child. When the baby comes, can Hedda really take care of it? She's so delusional that I'm afraid she'll get cloudy in her mind and try to harm the baby, even though she claims she loves him. It makes me think that someone should intervene."

"What do you mean?" An unsettling feeling seeped into Olivia's spirit.

"Maybe she needs some time away from the child when it's born. Maybe I could encourage her to stay in a mental-health facility for a while and let someone else take care of the baby." Noah looked at her suddenly.

"Listen to yourself." The hair on her arms bristled. "When you talk that way, it scares me. It's like I don't know you."

"Please don't say that. Of course you know me." He tried to take her in his arms, but she took a step back into a patch of shadow.

Was Noah worried about the baby because he was a caring man or because it was his child? And how could Noah send Hedda to one of those institutions—the place that he claimed killed his own mother? This tug-of-war in her emotions could drive her crazy if she let it.

Something hit the window, making them both startle.

"It must have been a bird. That happens sometimes." She looked out the window, searching the ground. A sparrow lay near a cluster of roses. The poor thing quivered and flapped around in a helpless circle, trying to get its strength back. In her youth, many times she'd felt just like that injured bird, frantic to fly away from Mrs. Adder's assaults.

Then suddenly the tiny beast fluttered and took off in the air. "Good," Olivia whispered more to herself than to Noah. "They're not always so fortunate. Sometimes they don't make it."

"This is not how I imagined this day would end. With Hedda at the helm of our lives. This is the worst day imaginable for me…and for you." His voice cracked. "I'm so sorry."

Oh, how she wanted to comfort him, but still questions pricked her like the sharp thorns on a rosebush. She ran her fingers along the windowsill—the very spot where Noah had entered the house for the first time— where he'd entered her life like a thief, stealing her heart. "I worry that the disloyalty that permeated this house while you were growing up is somehow coming back to haunt us." *That the seed of deception is in you as well as your parents.* "I want to believe you without reservation. I do with all of me, but…"

"But you can't?"

Olivia couldn't meet his eyes—those dark, searching eyes, seeking what she could no longer give freely, without reservation.

"Talk to me, my darling. Tell me everything that worries you."

Chapter 11

Darling? Noah had never called her by that name before, so it made her pause and stare at him. Search him. That word *darling* when he said it, the way he whispered it to her—warmed her through. Such intimacy, such heady romance. Only lovers of the greatest affection used that word. The word and the sweet way he wielded it made her move toward him against her will, against all her good sense.

Noah must have detected her melting resolve since he made up the distance between them in an instant.

They said nothing for a moment, and he didn't touch her, but his intention became clear.

Noah's breath tickled her cheek. He grazed his lips across her cheek and then hovered near her mouth.

The moment went soft and taut all at the same time.

Teasing and tender. Years fell from her as if she were young again and playful. Oh, how wonderful not to care about anything but the pleasures of life. To live in the moment, whatever it would bring. No hesitations. No regrets. What would that feel like? But her conscience, still strong and intact, niggled at her spirit. Just before their lips touched, Olivia whispered, "Why did you call me that?"

He grinned. "Call you what?"

"Why did you call me darling?"

Noah looked clueless. Had he already forgotten his term of endearment? Apparently guys who were smooth with the ladies could brandish that word along with the earnest men. She'd been like a child mesmerized by the treats in a candy store. Now Olivia could easily imagine Noah saying the word softly to Hedda. The beautiful, green-eyed Hedda. And, oh, how she must have swooned.

"Please tell me what you're thinking," Noah said. "I can't fight an invisible foe here." He tried on a grin, but the expression didn't fit him as well as it used to.

No matter how hard she rowed in the direction of reason and wisdom—and love—doubts consumed Olivia. Then they washed her over the edge like a rowboat falling over a waterfall. Finally Olivia said, "I was certain about Finney's character, and I was wrong. You were certain about your mother, and you were wrong. People lie. People cheat. Even good people. So, how can I be sure of anything anymore?"

"But I—"

"Let me finish," Olivia said, raising her voice. "Now

I must say the hardest thing of all. If what Hedda said is true about you…I'm saying *if*…then you're being like your mother in leading a double life with her numerous infidelities. And you're being like your father in convincing his loved one that she should be in a mental institution. Your father abandoned you because you weren't his own child, just as you are abandoning Hedda and the baby and wanting to secret her away to a mental institution—which, if I'm not mistaken, you called a prison!"

Noah let out a strange laugh. "Wow, those *are* hard things to hear, especially coming from you. To think you believe that I became the worst parts of Finney and my mother is quite a blow." The muscles on his jaw tightened.

"You said you wanted to know everything, and so there it is…*darling*." Hmm. She'd laced his sweet talk with sarcasm and then thrown it back in his face. Speaking her mind wasn't anything she was used to doing, but she'd learned that a wallflower would never grow—never bloom. It wasn't even real. So, even if she cringed later, Olivia wanted to lay it out now so they wouldn't take the chance of more regrets later on. "One last thing. I would pray long and hard about trying to take Hedda's child away from her…even for a while."

"I would, of course, use care, but what if Hedda were to become a caregiver like Mrs. Adder?" Noah asked. "Would you really want that? Especially when there was something we could have done about it?"

Noah had found her weakest link—the idea of creating another Mrs. Adder was an unthinkable prospect. And yet what Noah proposed concerning Hedda sounded equally frightening.

"I think we're both getting too tired to say much more," he said.

"Maybe."

"I'm heading back to the cottage soon. We should try to get a good night's sleep, since Hedda will be back tomorrow morning." Noah pointed toward her hand, the one fidgeting with the memory ribbon in her pocket. "May I have it…the ribbon?"

"Why do you need it?"

"To remind you of something."

She lifted the scarlet ribbon from her pocket and handed it to him.

Noah took hold of her hand and loosely twined the ribbon around her wrist. "I want you to remember my feelings for you tonight as you go to sleep. I want this to remind you of what we have together. Love is a bond strong enough to overcome doubt." He leaned toward her and whispered in her hair. "No matter what happens tomorrow…never forget."

What did Noah mean—*no matter what happens?* Would the truth come out then, and it wouldn't be in his favor? She wanted to pelt him with more queries, but she was too much of a coward to go on—afraid she might hear unhappy news. *Oh, dear Lord, help me.* Tears threatened, so she turned away. "Good night, Noah."

"Wait."

She glanced back at him. Noah's countenance was as heavy as her heart.

"You're not going to sneak off in the night, are you?" he asked.

"No, but…I could ask you the same question," Olivia said. "Vanishing when life gets tough is your forte, not mine." The moment the words were out of her mouth, she hated herself for them, especially when twinges of surprise and then sorrow streaked across his face.

"Yes. I deserved that…and more." He paused. "But please, promise me. I want to hear you say it. That you won't go." Noah reached out to her again and held her hand with fervor.

Running away was certainly easier. Perhaps she understood now why Noah had left all those years ago, and why it was so hard to come home. But she had been guilty of fleeing, as well—when they'd just met. To Noah's credit, he didn't mention her hasty withdrawal and return that first day. "I promise." No matter how much she wanted to stay within the warmth of his hand, she eased her hand from his grasp.

"Well, then, good night, my love."

"Good night." Olivia rushed out of the room as hot tears wet her skin. On her way up the staircase, she reached for the ribbon on her wrist. It was gone. It had only been loosely fastened to her wrist, so it must have fallen off when she fled the room. She searched the stairs and, when she couldn't find it, followed her steps back to the sunroom.

Noah hadn't left yet. He sat on a chair by the window, motionless. The scarlet ribbon streamed from his hand. Perhaps he thought that she had deliberately dropped the piece of trim to prove to him she no longer cared—that they were no longer bound by their tender devotion. It took every ounce of courage not to run to him and explain that it was she who wanted the ribbon tied on her wrist—securely, if need be—to remind her of his words, of his love. But there by the open door, something held her there. She couldn't move but, instead, watched as he began to weep. Did such strong emotion stem from the fallen ribbon and what it meant—or did it come from the consequences of falsehood and transgression?

When the last trace of twilight had given itself up to the darkness, Olivia still wasn't asleep. She rolled over in bed, punched her pillow a few times and stared into the lightless room. The ultraplush mattress had been good at wooing her body to sleep on previous nights, but it was easy to see that there would be none of that pleasantness tonight. At times, life felt like the reverse of an ultraplush mattress—more like a bed of nails. In fact, as the minutes ticked by, other issues of the day came into view. A truth, in fact. The Lord didn't always put people in one's path to bring a blessing. Many times it was the other way around—that He wanted to give people a chance to "be" the blessing.

The feverish look in Hedda's eyes plagued her. As terrible as the young woman's accusations were, there could be no denying her desperate need as she begged for help. That feeling Olivia knew well—too well. What it was like to cry out for help with no one to hear. For no one to care or notice. To be invisible.

Maybe God could redeem what had happened in her own youth with Mrs. Adder by giving her a heart for people who'd been abused by life. Maybe her unique upbringing could be used for something, for extending compassion. It had been so easy to hide through life, not only in her attic room, but in this house way out in the country. Even though it would be easier to be envious than compassionate concerning Hedda, it wasn't the way to go. It couldn't be. So, no matter whose baby Hedda carried, Olivia decided to help her. How she would do that, though, remained a mystery.

No matter how exhausted Olivia felt, sleep still wouldn't come, so she switched on her lamp and sat up for a while, swinging her legs over the bed. She picked up the photo of Noah, which she always kept on her nightstand. She'd long since removed the photo of the strangers—the people she'd pretended were her parents. With Noah, everything had changed. He'd filled that family void, and he'd made a place for himself in her frame as well as her heart.

She set the photo back down, went to the French doors and opened them to the balcony. There were a few stars peeking out here and there—the few that were brave enough to show themselves on such an anxious night—and the honeysuckle, which had become wild and seemed to grow just about everywhere, had loosed its scent in the air with abandon.

Olivia stepped out into the night and breathed deeply. She felt a stirring surrender in her spirit and whispered, "Oh, Lord Jesus, my own, You've not only been my savior, but You've been a good friend to me, the best, through the years. I would have died many a time if it hadn't been for Your mercy in staying the hand of Mrs.

Adder. I thank You for Your care in watching over my comings and goings. But I'm in the middle of a trial right now—a trial by fire. I know You are the master of redemption and that You promise to make good come out of man's evil and misfortune, so I ask You to be in our midst and bring great good out of these troubles. And allow me to help Hedda if that's what I'm to do."

Feeling some measure of peace and drowsiness, Olivia went back inside and climbed under the covers, leaving the French doors wide open to let in the night breezes. After an hour or so, she dipped into the bliss of sleep. Then suddenly, she awoke to the sound of popping and crackling. Olivia jerked up in bed. What was that sound? "Noah?" No one was there. The sound seemed to be coming from outside. Then an acrid odor stung her nostrils.

Smoke.

Something was burning. Had Hedda come back to burn the house down for revenge? *Oh, Lord, please don't let it be the manor!*

Olivia ran out onto the balcony. Noah stood on the ground below her. He was tending a small bonfire. What was he doing out there in the middle of the night? Not wanting to holler to him, she slipped on her robe and hurried down the stairs and out a side door. She approached him cautiously. "Noah?"

Noah glanced over at Olivia when she approached him by the fire. He had hoped she might hear the sputtering blaze and keep him company, but he didn't expect her to come. Not after such a shocking and stressful evening. "I couldn't sleep, so I decided to…" His voice faded. His strange midnight activities would require more explanation than he could muster at the moment.

"So, building bonfires is some new kind of sleeping aid?" Olivia gave him a nervous smile.

Normally he would have grinned, but his heart wasn't up to it.

"I see a few binders mixed in with the logs. It appears you're burning up your father's journals."

"That would be correct."

"Couldn't this have waited until tomorrow?"

"No." Noah poked at several of the logs on the fire to make them burn hotter.

"You could have just thrown them in the trash."

"You make it sound pretty easy."

"True. One time I think you said that advice flows more freely when it's not about your own life."

"Yeah, I would say something like that." He shrugged. "I guess I'm here because I don't trust myself. I would have kept dragging those journals out of the trash. This way, there's no turning back. I'll never be forced to look for any more pieces of the puzzle." His attention was pulled to a swarm of fireflies in a cluster of pines. He nodded toward the trees. "We have visitors." The lights looked like flashing bits of stardust. On any other night he would have marveled at the sight. But not tonight.

Olivia followed his gaze.

"Noah?"

"Yes?"

"Won't you regret this someday? You know, not reading all the journals?" Olivia's voice sounded full of sorrow for him.

"Maybe someday. Hard to know my mind years from now. But right now, all I feel is relief. That maybe what happened in the past will no longer have a hold on me. It's time to be my own man now...whoever that's supposed to be." Noah tossed the stick into the fire. "I've asked God about that very thing."

"And what did He say?"

"Not anything...yet." Several of the logs collapsed, making an explosion of tiny flares and sparkles. "But God has no problem talking through a burning bush, so I expect to hear from Him at any time." He gave her a weak smile.

"Is this connected to what happened today with Hedda?"

Noah pulled his harmonica out of his pocket but didn't play it. "In some ways, yes, but I'd been thinking of doing this for a while."

"I know you've gotten some bad news out of the journals, but—"

"It's more than that. I just couldn't take any more of their miseries. The bitterness in them. And then too, the more I read, the more I saw myself in those pages. You were right about me. I really was becoming the worst parts of Finney and my mother." A billow of smoke wafted over to them, and they backed away from the fire. "I've failed at so many things over the years. All the important things. If I'd been a fine enough man for you, you would have loved me. You would have believed me when I told you that I wasn't the father of Hedda's baby."

"You're mistaken." Olivia stepped toward him. "I do—"

"No," Noah said. "Please don't say it, even though I've prayed to hear it from you. Now it would seem I'd coerced you into saying it…out of pity. That is the one thing I can't take."

"But Noah?"

"Hmm?"

"You didn't even ask me about burning the journals. What if I'd wanted to read them…someday?"

Noah looked at her then. "I'm sorry this has hurt you. I really am." Perhaps her distant expression meant that she was adding this new pain to the pile of sufferings he'd brought into her life. To think he'd left Olivia out of the decision concerning the journals stabbed at his heart. He had thought only of himself. Would he ever be the man that Olivia deserved? Only God knew the answer to that one.

"Play something for me. Please?" Olivia said. "I think we need some music."

Noah paused for a moment to think of a song and then lifted his harmonica to his mouth to play "Somewhere Over the Rainbow." The melody danced around them even though his heart couldn't join in. While he played, Mops trotted over to join them. He didn't jump with his usual enthusiasm. Instead, he seemed to read their mood as he hunkered down between them, resting his head between his paws. Mops would wait with them through the night, which would surely be the longest of his life.

The next morning Olivia woke up early. The morning sunlight had already filtered through the plantation shutters, a rich light of many colors as if the clouds had leaked a bit of the heavens by accident. Perhaps the rays shone as a reminder that God was still in control of their destinies, not Hedda. Even though Olivia had gone to bed with a remnant of peace, some of the night's sleep had been fitful. Something had chased her on and off in strange bits of interconnected nightmares, but whatever the threat was had been engulfed in shadow.

Perhaps a fresh batch of fears had been tied to the nightmares, fears surrounding Noah's bonfire. It was impossible not to wonder if he'd been trying to dispose of the journals for other reasons. Maybe Finney had said something damaging about his son in his writings, things that Noah would never want her to know about, something that would fuel her reservations concerning their relationship. *Lord, I feel lost. Please give me discernment and wisdom, since I have never felt so lacking in either one.*

She glanced over at the clock. Seven. If she got up now, she'd have plenty of time to shower, dress and have breakfast before Hedda's arrival at nine.

Olivia rose from her bed and slipped into her house shoes—the ones that Noah had given her. When he'd found out that she'd never owned a pair of house shoes in her life, he'd driven into Gardenia to buy her some.

And then on another day he'd covered her bed with yellow rose petals. What a whimsical surprise that had been. Noah had simply said that maybe once in a while life really could be a bed of roses. Over the months, she'd discovered that Noah was full of those little kindnesses and thoughtful deeds. If those weren't enough fine qualities, he was also hardworking and romantic and funny. That was the Noah she'd grown to love.

She'd become such a mess of emotions, tossed back and forth on the waves of love and fear—and doubt. It was obvious that creation had fallen into chaos, like a perfect blue marble shattered into a million pieces. And there would be more of those pieces to deal with this very morning.

At fifteen minutes before nine, Noah came over to the big house to be with Olivia as they waited for Hedda to arrive. As soon as he sat down in the front living room, he said, "I've made a decision. When Hedda arrives, we should offer her help, whether she admits that she's lying about the baby or not. Instead of suggesting that she voluntarily admit herself to a mental-health facility, I'll offer her some kind of assistance. Not sure what that entails yet, but I'll think of something. I know that to ever be worthy of your love, I'll need to start thinking of someone besides myself."

"Perhaps it's providence, since yesterday I had come to the same conclusion. Maybe we—"

The doorbell rang.

Noah glanced over at Olivia. "It's going to be okay. I promise."

As he opened the door, they stood side by side.

Hedda stood on the welcome mat looking miserable.

"Hi," Noah said. "Won't you come in?"

She looked back and forth at them like a scared animal, and yet she also looked ready to pounce. Hedda stepped inside the entry.

Noah closed the door and gestured for her to sit in the front living room.

When the three of them were seated, Hedda fiddled with the ruffles on her blouse and said, "I like this room. On the outside, it's a grand and glorious turret, but on the inside, well, it's a cozy alcove…a place to feel at home." She pressed her finger against her temple. "Amazing how things can seem one way but really be another."

Noah tensed. "Whatever you need to—"

"Would you like something to drink?" Olivia asked, deliberately interrupting Noah, hoping he'd be able to remain calm. "Some tea or coffee?"

"No. Nothing. Thanks." Hedda frowned at Olivia. "Why are you being so nice to me?"

Noah leaned forward, resting his arms on his knees. "Olivia and I would like to help you."

"But what does Olivia have to do with us?" Hedda squirmed on the velvet chair. "Is this a trick to get me to go away?" She held on to her purse strap like a lifeline.

Noah cleared his throat. "If you feel the father of your child or your family isn't going to support you in this, then we will do what we can. We won't walk away from you."

"This *is* a trick," Hedda said.

Noah took in a deep breath and let it out slowly. "I do want to help you. The only thing I can't do is to lie about what happened. But it's obvious that you're in trouble, so—"

"I'm in trouble because of you." Hedda slammed her purse on the coffee table.

"I'm sorry." Noah put up his hands. "Bad choice of words. If you have some need, we're here for you."

"That doesn't sound like love." Hedda asked, "Are you going to give me a payoff?"

"No." Noah closed his eyes for a second as if to pray. "We can put you in touch with a place that will help unmarried women in your condition, and whatever they don't supply in baby items, we can help fill in the gaps. You won't be alone in this."

"And I'd be happy to help babysit in emergencies," Olivia said.

"We both will. I did check some online places in Houston, and there really are a lot of centers that help women—"

"Yes, I heard you." Hedda rose off the chair. "Women like me…unmarried women in trouble. You're an unmarried man in trouble, but no one seems to care. Has society changed so little in the past decades in the way it treats unwed mothers versus unwed fathers? Besides, I wouldn't be an unmarried woman in trouble if you would do the right thing and marry me."

"Hedda, we really are trying here," Noah said, "but you're going to have to—"

"I don't have to do anything. And it's tearing me to pieces the way you're making me sound so…dirty."

Now Olivia had to pray for patience. "Hedda," Olivia said. "No one wants to make you feel—"

"Please stop," Hedda said to Olivia. "After all, you're the 'other' woman, not me."

Noah got up from the couch. "I will not allow you to speak to—"

"No more." Hedda covered her ears with her hands. "I won't listen to any more of your lies. I know what I have to do. It's not my fault. It's yours. You've driven me to it." She edged away from her chair and into the entry hall. "You'll see." Hedda's eyes flashed anger, and then they glazed into an unreadable expression. "You'll see."

Noah took a step toward her. "Driven you to do what?"

"Don't try to stop me. I know where your balcony is." Hedda turned and ran toward the staircase.

Chapter 12

Noah ran to the front door and called back to Olivia. "Go to the balcony and try to stop her. I'm going to stand outside and try to catch her if she jumps." The last he saw of Olivia's face was her look of terror as she ran after Hedda. *God help her not to jump!*

Noah made it underneath the balcony just as Hedda leaned over the iron railing. "Don't do it. Please. I beg you."

"Then tell me the truth," Hedda called down to him. "Tell me you love me. Tell me you're the father of my child." She leaned so far forward that her body teetered on the iron balustrade.

"No. Please! All right," he said, stumbling back on the rocks. "Yes. I'm the child's father, and I love you." The sound of his own voice saying the words sounded hollow—as empty as a sail on a windless day. *God, forgive me for the lies, but how else can I save her and the baby?* "Now please come down."

Hedda spread her arms as though she could fly. "If I had fallen just now, I might have died...just like you."

What was going on in Hedda's mind? "What do you mean I died?" Noah asked, bewildered.

"In the letter to your father ten years ago. Your father thought you were dead, and so it was true. At least it was to him."

"You?" Noah staggered backward. "So, it was you who wrote that letter to my father, telling him I'd died?"

"I did."

"But why? Hedda, why would you do such a thing?" He wanted to shout at her, but he didn't want to send her into another panic.

"To punish you, of course. I gave you my love...all that I had. And you paid me back by walking away as if I were nobody to you. As if I meant nothing. So, someone had to teach you a lesson. Not to hide your love."

"Hedda." That made no sense. Noah raised his hands to her. What could he say? Was she merely unbalanced or evil—or both? His head swam with the revelation. He wanted to tell her all the miseries that her lie had unleashed over the years—a domino effect of confusion and grief—but since she was so close to destroying herself and the baby, he would let it go—for now. "We can talk about this later. Come down now. If you jump, you will be severely injured and your baby will most certainly die. And I know you're not a murderer."

"A murderer?" she called down to him. "That's impossible now."

"Hedda, please talk to me clearly. I don't understand you."

"My child…our baby…is already dead!" Hedda pounded her fists on the iron. "I miscarried last night. Our child has gone to be with God. But too early to go home. Much too early." She mumbled some words that he couldn't make out, but anguish darkened her features.

Lord, have mercy on us. Why hadn't Hedda told him this morning that she'd miscarried? Why had she continued with the charade? She was surely distraught and deeply disturbed. *But, Lord, what can I do for her? How can we help her?*

"This morning I buried him in the woods by my house…near an old oak tree. He was so tiny in my hands, but perfect and beautiful like a tiny porcelain figurine. If he had lived, he would have been one of the greatest joys of my life."

"I'm so sorry." Noah pressed his palm over his chest to calm his heart.

"I wanted to love a child and to be loved, but now that has all been taken away from me. But there is love after all. You did say it. I heard you. You said you loved me. So, I forgive you for walking away…for hiding your love."

"I care about you, and if you care anything about me, you won't jump. There's so much more to your life. You shouldn't throw it away. It's too precious. Please, I want you to come down. Right now." Noah could hear

Olivia talking to her, begging her to come inside, but Hedda ignored all her pleadings.

"Yes, yes. I will come down. Now. Yes, if you truly love me then you'll be able to catch me."

"No!" Noah yelled to her.

Hedda spread her arms out straight as she leaned perilously over the railing. For a second her body teetered.

Olivia ran out onto the balcony and grabbed at Hedda's long skirt. The fabric tore as Hedda toppled over the edge screaming.

In those frantic two seconds, Noah tried to position himself so he could catch her. Hedda slammed against him, landing hard in his arms. The blow knocked him over, making them both collapse on the rocky ground. The side of his body and face crashed against some stones. Hedda let out a moan, but he could no longer feel her in his arms. His mouth filled with the taste of blood.

"Hard to breathe," he said. His chest became like iron. Sounds thundered around him and then became muffled, as if he'd traveled through a tunnel. The last things he could make out were Mops licking his hand and Olivia's panicked voice above him.

Then life faded into blackness.

Noah was in a profound sleep when Olivia arrived in one of the observation rooms, just outside the E.R. Pleased that he was resting, she went in search of Hedda. When she saw her through the glass door, Olivia paused before going inside. What could she possibly say to the poor woman? Noah had been right. Hedda really was deeply troubled in her mind—more so than she'd realized. The woman was in need of serious counseling and medicine. Perhaps the events of the day would have turned out differently if she hadn't made Noah feel guilty about his suggestion that Hedda go to a mental-health facility. There was no way to know the outcome, but maybe if they'd approached Hedda in a different way, she wouldn't have jumped. There wouldn't have been such a tragic end to the day.

Olivia took in a deep breath and slid open the glass door. The woman, now ashen pale, was covered right up to her neck with the hospital sheet. Monitors beeped, sounding menacing, while the antiseptic smells prickled her senses. She never had liked hospitals. It meant that life was off-kilter again, and people were suffering.

Hedda's eyes opened.

"Hi. I came to check on you," Olivia said. "I'm so sorry you lost your baby yesterday."

"Me too." Hedda reached up and yanked the oxygen tubes out of her nose.

"Is it okay to do that?"

Hedda shrugged and then touched her bandaged head. "My mind feels like it's emerging from a fog. They have something in my IV. It's probably the medication I'd been denying myself. But along with my new clarity is depression. Feels pretty bad…because now I can see what I've done. The mess I've made. The pain I've caused," she murmured as if speaking to the air.

"You don't have to talk about it…unless you want to."

"I guess I should talk about it. My brain felt weary from trying to decipher what is real and what isn't. This fog…well, it was dreamlike, but not in a good way. It was like watching myself from afar. I could see myself saying things and doing things, but I couldn't always know who was speaking…me or someone like me. Another part of me. Does that make any sense?" She released a mirthless chuckle. "It barely makes sense to me."

Olivia placed her hands on the bed rail. "I'm sure it was frightening to feel those things."

"My life has never been easy. Ever since I was a kid, I've craved love like some people crave heroin. I had a taste of love with Noah, or at least his affection, and then he walked away. He took away my high. I lost my mind for a while. But I can't blame him. I would have walked away from me, too. You two couldn't possibly hate me more than I do."

"We don't hate you." Olivia touched her arm.

"Well, not being hated isn't as good as being loved… but maybe it's a start." Hedda fumbled for a box of tissues on the bed table but couldn't quite reach it.

Olivia eased the box closer to her. "You must have had a terrible childhood."

Hedda plucked a few tissues out of the box. "Classic dysfunctional family. Alcoholic mother and absent father. I don't remember many easy days. I remember the blur between reality and fantasy even as a child. I know it was a way to protect myself from the pain…to disconnect from it." She seemed to study Olivia's face. "I know someone like you couldn't imagine what I'm talking about."

"I know a little of what you're saying." Olivia wasn't sure how much to reveal about her past. But why should she be so private if it could help Hedda? "I grew up in a foster home, and my caregiver was abusive. I never had a real home, and I knew what loneliness was." Mrs. Adder and her sneering lies were always echoing in her thoughts, but she also knew God wouldn't want her to think of herself as useless and unfit to be loved. In an act of will, Olivia denounced all of Mrs. Adder's influence over her life. *No more.* From here on out, as best she could, she would embrace the knowledge that she was God's own and she was loved.

"Loneliness can eat away at a person like acid." Hedda rested her head back on the pillow, and a little stream of tears trickled from her eyes into her hair. "Guess I've always been short on friends."

Olivia had no idea where her offer might lead her, but she was determined to make it. "I'd like to be your friend…if it's okay with you."

"You want to be my friend after all I did to you and Noah?"

"Yes."

"Then you're as crazy as I am." She choked out a laugh.

Olivia chuckled along with her.

"Just like that? Humph. Well, we'll see." A new batch of tears came, and Hedda wiped at her face with the tissues. "While I was lying here, watching the drips and that clock over there ticking my miserable life away, I decided something…that I need help. For the first time, I'm going to get counseling, and I'm going to be accountable to someone about my meds."

"That sounds good. I'll pray that it all goes well. If

you want me to go with you to an appointment, I'd be happy to be there for support."

"I might take you up on it." Hedda caressed her belly, and then, as if remembering her loss, she sighed.

Olivia's heart went out to the woman. Such a great loss had to be hard. *Oh, Lord, please let Hedda recover and find a good life with You by her side.*

"I do have one thing else to say." She let her hand flop back on the bed as if what she had to say would take all her remaining strength. "His name was Terrell Mulligan."

"Who?"

Hedda ran her fingers along the edge of the sheet, pulling it taut. "Terrell Mulligan is the man I slept with." With a sudden air of determination, she looked at Olivia straight on and said, "The baby I miscarried belonged to a man named Terrell…not Noah.

"I see the questions all over your face," Hedda continued. "Let me just say that Terrell didn't love me. Our relationship was hopeless right from the start. But I guess I've learned the hard way that getting pregnant isn't a good way to make a man marry you, and threatening a man isn't the right way to make him fall in love with you."

Hedda rolled her head back and forth on the pillow and groaned. "What was I thinking, except to be out of my mind? Yes, of course." She rolled her eyes. "Anyway, everything Noah said was true. He *is* a good man, but you already know that. And we found out today that he's willing to risk his life to help a fool. You know, most people manage to make a ruin of their lives from time to time, but I've taken it to a much higher level. I'm the queen of fools."

"Please don't be so hard on yourself." Olivia reached over to Hedda and squeezed her hand. "It's okay. No one has escaped the ruins." *Especially when I stubbornly chose not to believe Noah's side of the story.* Such unnecessary suffering by her own hand.

"The nurse told me that Noah was all right. That he would recover. But tell him how sorry I am…for everything. Tell him I understand if he can't forgive me."

"I'll tell him, and I'm sure he will forgive you."

Hedda scooted down in the bed and reached for the blanket.

Olivia lifted the coverlet around Hedda and gingerly tucked her in.

"Funny thing. I never remember my mom doing that. You know, tucking me in. She was always too occupied… with her bottle."

"I'm so sorry."

"Yeah, me too."

"I hope you can get some rest now. I'll come back in to check on you before I go."

"Okay." Hedda gave her a feeble smile, but it was still a smile.

Then she closed her eyes, and Olivia stepped out into the hallway.

Moments later, when Olivia walked into Noah's room, he put on a wide smile. He tried to rise up on his arm to show her how thrilled he was to see her, but pain sent him crumpling back into the bed.

"Please don't get up." Olivia went to him and gently touched his shoulder. "I'll come to you. Is it okay if I hug you?"

"I'll always be well enough for your embrace, my love."

She lowered herself to him and, with great care, placed her arms around him. "You are such a hero. *My* hero. But, Noah, you could have broken your neck."

"I'll be fine. Only bruises and some cracked ribs."

"Ow. Listen to the sound of that. It's awful." Olivia eased away to look at him.

"I'll survive this. We all will."

"I saw Hedda just now. She has some injuries, but the doctor says she'll recover just fine."

"The doctor told me," he said. "I'm glad she'll be okay. That's very good news."

"In fact, Noah, she was lucid in her thinking and speaking. It's just that now, well, she's suffering from depression, because she knows clearly what she's done. All the lies. She told me that you weren't the father, and she's asked you to forgive her...for everything."

"I do forgive her. And I'm sorry she lost the baby. I know that must only add to her depression."

"It does," Olivia said, "but I think she's going to be okay now. She admitted that she needs counseling."

"Good. Sounds like you two had quite a chat."

"We did." Olivia dug around in her purse and pulled out his harmonica. "Just in case you need it." She set it on the bed table.

"I'm not sure I can breathe that deeply yet, but thanks. I'm glad to have all the things that I love near me. I'll heal faster that way." He gave her a tentative smile.

"Noah?"

"Hmm?"

She moved a strand of his hair away from his forehead. "Can you ever forgive me for not trusting you? For doubting your love? It was so wrong of me. You needed loyalty, and I gave you sorrow. I want to cry every time I think of all the cruel things I said to you in the sunroom yesterday."

"Which cruel words?" Noah said, grinning. "There were so many."

Olivia's chin started to quiver.

"I was just teasing you, but I shouldn't have." He shook his head. "It's too soon for any of this to be funny. I'm sorry."

"You must think I'm a—"

Noah touched his finger to her lips. "Shh. Everything is all right."

"But I nearly messed things up between us. I almost…" She released a little sob. "I need to hear the actual words if it's okay. That you're willing to forgive me."

"Come here." Noah pulled her to him. "You are forgiven." He breathed her in, grateful for the moment. "I love you so much."

"And I you."

"But I need to hear the actual words, if it's okay."

"I love you, Noah Bromfeld. I love you so," Olivia said. "You know, I've heard love referred to as a sweet affliction. If that's true, then I have a terminal case of it."

Noah laughed and then winced.

"Ow. I'm sure that hurt. I'll try not to say anything funny."

"You say whatever you like, but I have something that needs to be said. I'm sorry I never told you about Hedda. I was trying to save you from worry, but it wasn't honest. It wasn't right."

"No need for you to ask for forgiveness."

Noah kissed her on the head and then eased her up to kiss her good and proper on the lips. "Now can we have a talk…about us?"

"Yes. Oh, yes."

"Well, first things first. We have a legal problem."

"What?"

Noah smiled.

"I see that twinkle again. So, what is our legal problem?"

"No one really owns Bromfeld Manor. You do, but you keep refusing it. So, I have a plan for how to fix that. I would have told you sooner except that Lucile kept getting in the way." Noah grimaced and pretended to look over her shoulder. "She's not here, is she?"

Olivia chuckled. "No."

"Good. That's excellent news," he said. "Sorry. I know you're fond of her."

"It's okay. Now tell me your plan before you forget it or we're interrupted by some overenthusiastic nurse who wants to take your vitals."

Noah took her hand in his. "The plan is simple, but it does take a yes. A very important yes that has to come from you."

Olivia gave his hand a squeeze. "And what might that question be?"

"Will you finally accept Bromfeld Manor as your home...if I offer it to you as a wedding gift?"

"I don't know." Olivia arched her brow. "It depends on whose wedding it is."

"Yours...mine...ours."

"*Ours* is one of the most romantic words in the dictionary."

"It is," Noah said. "I can't imagine my life with anyone else but you. So, will you be my wife?"

"Yes. Oh, yes. I will be your wife."

"'Mrs. Olivia Bromfeld' has a nice sound to it."

"It does indeed, Mr. Bromfeld."

"So, tell me, my darling, is this a paint-the-house-purple kind of moment?"

She touched her forehead to his. "I think it deserves a whole rainbow, don't you?"

"It would if I had your ring with me, and if we were in a more romantic setting instead of being serenaded by heart monitors. *And* if I was dressed in a suit instead of a backless hospital gown."

Olivia eased away, laughing. Strands of her hair caught on the stubble on his face.

Noah scrubbed his fist along his chin. "Look at me. I'm a mess."

"Yes, you are quite the wonderful mess. But don't you see? I'm just glad you're alive. That's enough for me to celebrate."

"But I *will* take you into the city to celebrate."

"And I *will* be happy to go."

Noah raised his hand, since that was one of the only things that didn't hurt, and Olivia placed her hand against his. They laced their fingers together. "We fit so perfectly together."

Olivia leaned down again, and Noah buried his face in the folds of her hair. *What joy to be near her all the remaining days of my life.* After a moment he said softly, "A novelist, I think George Moore, once wrote, 'A man travels the world over in search of what he needs and returns home to find it.' And that, for me, couldn't be more true."

"Oh?" Olivia lifted up to look at him. "I want to know more."

"Well, even when I was traipsing around aimlessly on the other side of this planet, you were right here… all along." Noah kissed the tip of her nose. "I think this moment has been a smile in God's heart for a long time. He could see what I couldn't…that love would bring me home at last."

* * * * *

REQUEST YOUR FREE BOOKS!

2 FREE INSPIRATIONAL NOVELS
PLUS 2
FREE
MYSTERY GIFTS

Love Inspired

YES! Please send me 2 FREE Love Inspired® novels and my 2 FREE mystery gifts (gifts are worth about $10). After receiving them, if I don't wish to receive any more books, I can return the shipping statement marked "cancel." If I don't cancel, I will receive 6 brand-new novels every month and be billed just $4.74 per book in the U.S. or $5.24 per book in Canada. That's a savings of at least 21% off the cover price. It's quite a bargain! Shipping and handling is just 50¢ per book in the U.S. and 75¢ per book in Canada.* I understand that accepting the 2 free books and gifts places me under no obligation to buy anything. I can always return a shipment and cancel at any time. Even if I never buy another book, the two free books and gifts are mine to keep forever.

105/305 IDN F49N

Name   (PLEASE PRINT)

Address   Apt. #

City   State/Prov.   Zip/Postal Code

Signature (if under 18, a parent or guardian must sign)

Mail to the Harlequin® Reader Service:
IN U.S.A.: P.O. Box 1867, Buffalo, NY 14240-1867
IN CANADA: P.O. Box 609, Fort Erie, Ontario L2A 5X3

**Are you a subscriber to Love Inspired books
and want to receive the larger-print edition?
Call 1-800-873-8635 or visit www.ReaderService.com.**

* Terms and prices subject to change without notice. Prices do not include applicable taxes. Sales tax applicable in N.Y. Canadian residents will be charged applicable taxes. Offer not valid in Quebec. This offer is limited to one order per household. Not valid for current subscribers to Love Inspired books. All orders subject to credit approval. Credit or debit balances in a customer's account(s) may be offset by any other outstanding balance owed by or to the customer. Please allow 4 to 6 weeks for delivery. Offer available while quantities last.

Your Privacy—The Harlequin® Reader Service is committed to protecting your privacy. Our Privacy Policy is available online at www.ReaderService.com or upon request from the Harlequin Reader Service.
We make a portion of our mailing list available to reputable third parties that offer products we believe may interest you. If you prefer that we not exchange your name with third parties, or if you wish to clarify or modify your communication preferences, please visit us at www.ReaderService.com/consumerchoice or write to us at Harlequin Reader Service Preference Service, P.O. Box 9062, Buffalo, NY 14269. Include your complete name and address.

LIDIR13R

REQUEST YOUR FREE BOOKS!

2 FREE INSPIRATIONAL NOVELS
PLUS 2
FREE
MYSTERY GIFTS

Love Inspired
HISTORICAL
INSPIRATIONAL HISTORICAL ROMANCE

LIHDIR13R